ANGELS in AMERICA

A Gay Fantasia on National Themes

PART TWO: PERESTROIKA

Tony Kushner

With an Afterword by the Author

Theatre Communications Group

Kushner, Tony.
    Angels in America.
    Contents: pt. 1. Millennium approaches—pt. 2. Perestroika.
    1. Cohn, Roy M.—Drama. 2. Gay men—United States—
Drama. I. Title.
PS3561.U778A85   1993   812′.54   92-44011
ISBN 1-55936-060-7 (cloth : v. 1)
ISBN 1-55936-061-5 (pbk. : v. 1)
ISBN 1-55936-072-0 (cloth : v. 2)
ISBN 1-55936-073-9 (pbk. : v. 2)

Book design and composition by The Sarabande Press

First Edition, February 1994
Second Printing, April 1994
Third Printing, August 1994
Fourth Printing, November 1994
Fifth Printing, June 1995

The actors, directors and designers who have worked on the play transformed it. What follows is a list of the play's productions to date.

Perestroika was first performed as a staged reading in conjunction with the production of *Millennium Approaches* presented by the Eureka Theatre Company in San Francisco, May 1991. Both reading and production were directed by David Esbjornson. Sets were designed by Tom Kamm, costumes by Sandra Woodall and lights by Jack Carpenter and Jim Cave. The cast was as follows:

THE ANGEL	*Ellen McLaughlin*
PRIOR WALTER	*Stephen Spinella*
LOUIS IRONSON	*Michael Ornstein*
JOE PITT	*Michael Scott Ryan*
HARPER PITT	*Anne Darragh*
HANNAH PITT	*Kathleen Chalfant*
BELIZE	*Harry Waters Jr.*
ROY COHN	*John Bellucci*

The play was further developed in workshop and presented as a staged reading at the Mark Taper Forum in Los Angeles, May 1992. The workshop and reading were directed by Oskar Eustis and Tony Taccone. The cast was as follows:

THE ANGEL	*Ellen McLaughlin*
PRIOR WALTER	*Stephen Spinella*
LOUIS IRONSON	*Joe Mantello*
JOE PITT	*Jeffrey King*
HARPER PITT	*Cynthia Mace*
HANNAH PITT	*Kathleen Chalfant*
BELIZE	*Harry Waters Jr.*
ROY COHN	*Larry Pressman*

The world premiere of *Perestroika* was presented by the Mark Taper Forum, November 1992, directed by Oskar Eustis and Tony Taccone, with sets designed by John Conklin, lights by Pat Collins, costumes by Gabriel Berry and music by Mel Marvin. The cast was as follows:

THE ANGEL	*Ellen McLaughlin*
PRIOR WALTER	*Stephen Spinella*
LOUIS IRONSON	*Joe Mantello*
JOE PITT	*Jeffrey King*
HARPER PITT	*Cynthia Mace*
HANNAH PITT	*Kathleen Chalfant*
BELIZE	*K. Todd Freeman*
ROY COHN	*Ron Leibman*

The play was presented by New York University/Tisch School of the Arts, April 1993. It was directed by Michael Mayer, with sets by Tony Cisek and Andrew Hall, lights by Jack Mehler, costumes by Robin J. Orloff and music by Michael Ward. The cast was as follows:

THE ANGEL	*Jenna Stern*
PRIOR WALTER	*Daniel Zelman*
LOUIS IRONSON	*Johnny Garcia*
JOE PITT	*Robert Carin*
HARPER PITT	*Debra Messing*
HANNAH PITT	*Vivienne Benesch*
BELIZE	*Mark Douglas*
ROY COHN	*Ben Schenkman*

The play opened in London on November 20, 1993 in a production at the Royal National Theatre of Great Britain, directed by Declan Donellan, designed by Nick Ormerod, with lights by Mick Hughes and music by Paddy Cuneen. The cast was as follows:

PRELAPSARIANOV/THE RABBI	*Harry Towb*
THE ANGEL	*Nancy Crane*
PRIOR WALTER	*Stephen Dillane*
LOUIS IRONSON	*Jason Isaacs*
JOE PITT	*Daniel Craig*
HARPER PITT	*Clare Holman*
HANNAH PITT	*Susan Engel*
BELIZE	*Joseph Mydell*
ROY COHN	*David Schofield*

Perestroika opened in New York at the Walter Kerr Theatre on November 23, 1993, in a production directed by George C. Wolfe with sets by Robin Wagner, lights by Jules Fisher, costumes by Toni-Leslie James and music by Anthony Davis. The cast was as follows:

THE ANGEL	*Ellen McLaughlin*
PRIOR WALTER	*Stephen Spinella*
LOUIS IRONSON	*Joe Mantello*
JOE PITT	*David Marshall Grant*
HARPER PITT	*Marcia Gay Harden*
HANNAH PITT	*Kathleen Chalfant*
BELIZE	*Jeffrey Wright*
ROY COHN	*Ron Leibman*

ACKNOWLEDGMENTS

I've been working on *Perestroika* since 1989. In the process I've accumulated many debts:

Abundant support, both financial and emotional, was provided by my parents, Bill and Sylvia Kushner, and my aunt Martha Deutscher. My father has been terrifically helpful as *Perestroika* has come to completion.

My brother and sister, Eric and Lesley Kushner, have supported me both in my work and in the difficult process of coming out; without their love and enthusiasm writing this would never have been possible. The same is true for Mark Bronnenberg, to whom *Millennium Approaches* was dedicated.

Dot and Jerry Edelstien, and Marcia, Tony and Alex Cunha made homes away from home for me.

Jim Nicola of New York Theatre Workshop has encouraged and advised me all the way, and so has Rosemarie Tichler of the New York Shakespeare Festival. Together they shed blood for the play, literally; they have won my purple heart.

Joyce Ketay, the Wonder-Agent, and her associate Carl Mulert, have been incredible friends and guardians. Michael

Petshaft makes life seem manageable and has helped me keep sane.

Gordon Davidson has been the most open-hearted and -handed producer/shepherd any playwright could ever want, and the whole staff of the Taper has been sensational, fabulous, divine.

The National Theatre staff has also been immensely supportive; and I am particularly grateful to Richard Eyre and Giles Croft for believing in the play even in its scruffiest stages.

I am also indebted to Rocco Landesman, Jack Viertel, Paul Libin, Margo Lion, Susan Gallin, Herb Alpert, Fred Zollo and the angelic hosts of brave and honorable producers who gambled on this outrageous experiment on Broadway.

Mary K. Klinger stage managed the show both in Los Angeles and in New York, unshakable in the face of many tempests.

The play has benefited from the dramaturgical work of Leon Katz and K.C. Davis, as well as the directors and actors who have participated in its various workshops and productions.

Stephen Spinella, Joe Mantello and particularly Ellen McLaughlin have made invaluable suggestions on shaping and editing.

Sigrid Wurschmidt, actress extraordinaire and angel of light, remains with the play though she's left the world.

David Esbjornson, who directed the play in its first draft in San Francisco, has listened to and commented on its stories ever since.

Tony Taccone made invaluable structuring suggestions during his work on the play in Los Angeles.

Declan Donellan and Nick Ormerod directed and designed the play at the National Theatre in London. Their early insights and responses have been challenging and helpful and have goaded me to keep trying to make the play better.

George C. Wolfe has been an inspiring and indefatigable collaborator on this final stage of shaping the script; he's been brilliantly insightful, respectful and galvanizing. The last step was the hardest, and I wouldn't have managed it without him.

Oskar Eustis commissioned *Angels in America* and has been intimately involved in every stage of its development. Without his great intelligence, talent, friendship and determination, the project would have been neither begun nor completed. I began *Angels* as a conversation, real and imaginary, between Oskar and myself; that conversation has never stopped, and I hope never will.

A few months after I started work on *Perestroika* my mother died of cancer. She's a mighty presence in the play.

In the fifteen years of our friendship Kimberly T. Flynn has taught me much of what I now believe to be true about life: theory and practice. Her words and ideas are woven through the work, and our life together is its bedrock. *Perestroika* is for Kimberly. This is her play as much as it is mine.

Angels in America

The Characters

THE ANGEL, *four divine emanations, Fluor, Phosphor, Lumen and Candle; manifest in One: the Continental Principality of America. She has magnificent gray steel wings.*

PRIOR WALTER, *Louis's abandoned boyfriend. Before discovering that he has AIDS, worked occasionally as a club designer or caterer. Mostly lives modestly off a small trust fund.*

LOUIS IRONSON, *a word processor working for the Second Circuit Court of Appeals.*

JOSEPH PORTER PITT, *chief clerk for Justice Theodore Wilson of the Federal Court of Appeals, Second Circuit.*

HARPER AMATY PITT, *Joe's wife, an agoraphobic with a mild Valium addiction and a much stronger imagination.*

HANNAH PORTER PITT, *Joe's mother, formerly of Salt Lake City, now staying in Brooklyn. Lives off her deceased husband's army pension.*

BELIZE, *a former drag queen and former lover of Prior's. A registered nurse. Belize's name was originally Norman Arriaga; Belize is a drag name that stuck.*

ROY M. COHN, *a successful New York lawyer and unofficial power broker, now facing disbarment and dying of AIDS.*

Other Characters in Part Two

ALEKSII ANTEDILLUVIANOVICH PRELAPSARIANOV, *the World's Oldest Bolshevik, played by the actress playing Hannah.*

MR. LIES, *Harper's imaginary friend, a travel agent, who in style of dress and speech suggests a jazz musician; he always wears a large lapel badge emblazoned "IOTA" (The International Order of Travel Agents). He is played by the actor playing Belize.*

HENRY, *Roy's doctor, played by the actress playing Hannah.*

ETHEL ROSENBERG, *played by the actress playing Hannah.*

EMILY, *a nurse, played by the actress playing the Angel.*

Mannequins in the Diorama Room of the Mormon Visitors' Center:

THE MORMON FATHER, *played by the actor playing Joe.*

CALEB, *an offstage voice; the voice of the actor playing Belize.*

ORRIN, *an offstage voice; the voice of the actress playing the Angel.*

THE MORMON MOTHER, *played by the actress playing the Angel.*

The Continental Principalities, *inconceivably powerful Celestial Apparatchik/Bureaucrat-Angels of whom the Angel of America is a peer:*

THE ANGEL EUROPA, *played by the actor playing Joe.*

THE ANGEL AFRICANII, *played by the actress playing Harper.*

THE ANGEL OCEANIA, *played by the actor playing Belize.*

THE ANGEL ASIATICA, *played by the actress playing Hannah.*

THE ANGEL AUSTRALIA, *played by the actor playing Louis.*

THE ANGEL ANTARCTICA, *played by the actor playing Roy.*

4

RABBI ISIDOR CHEMELWITZ, *an orthodox Jewish rabbi, played by the actress playing Hannah.*

SARAH IRONSON, *Louis's dead grandma, who was interred by Rabbi Chemelwitz in Part One, Act One. She is played by the actor playing Louis.*

TAPED VOICE: *The voice that introduces Prelapsarianov in Act One Scene 1 and the Council of Principalities in Act Five Scene 5, and that speaks the welcome and narrative introduction in the diorama, should be that of the actress playing the Angel. These taped intros should sound alike: not parodic but beautiful and serious, the way the unseen Angel sounds in* Millennium.

Playwright's notes

A DISCLAIMER: Roy M. Cohn, the character, is based on the late Roy M. Cohn (1927-1986), who was all too real; for the most part the acts attributed to the character Roy are to be found in the historical record. But this Roy is a work of dramatic fiction; his words are my invention, and liberties have been taken with his story. The real Roy died in August of 1986. For purposes of the play my Roy dies in February.

I want to acknowledge my indebtedness to Harold Bloom's reading of the Jacob story, which I first encountered in his introduction to Olivier Revault D'Allones's *Musical Variations on Jewish Thought*, in which Bloom translates the Hebrew word for "blessing" as "more life." Bloom expands on his interpretation in *The Book of J*.

Yiddish translation was graciously provided by Joachim Neugroschel, and additionally by Jeffrey Salant.

Ian Kramer, Esq. provided essential information about the juridical mischief of the Reagan-era federal bench. The court cases in Act Four Scene 8 are actual cases with some of the names and circumstances changed.

A NOTE ABOUT THE STAGING: The play benefits from a pared-down style of presentation, with minimal scenery and scene shifts done rapidly (no blackouts!) employing the cast as well as stagehands—which makes for an actor-driven event, as this must be. The moments of magic—all of them—are to be fully realized, as bits of wonderful *theatrical* illusion—which means it's OK if the wires show, and maybe it's good that they do, but the magic should at the same time be thoroughly amazing.

It should also be said that *Millennium Approaches* and *Perestroika* are very different plays, and if one is producing them in repertory the difference should be reflected in their designs. *Perestroika* proceeds forward from the wreckage made by the Angel's traumatic entry at the end of *Millennium*. A membrane has broken; there is disarray and debris.

Perestroika is essentially a comedy, in that issues are re-solved, mostly peaceably, growth takes place and loss is, to a certain degree, countenanced. But it's not a farce; all this happens only through a terrific amount of struggle, and the stakes are high. The angel, the scenes in Heaven, Prior's prophet scenes are not lapses into some sort of elbow-in-the-ribs playing style. The angel is immensely august, serious and dangerously powerful *always*, and Prior is running for his life, sick, scared and alone. Every moment must be played for its reality, the terms always life and death; only then will the comedy emerge. There is also a danger in easy sentiment. Eschew sentiment! Particularly in the final act—metaphorical though it may at times be (or maybe not), the problems the characters face are finally among the hardest problems—how to let go of the past, how to change and lose with grace, how to keep going in the face of overwhelming suffering. It shouldn't be easy.

THE ANGEL'S COUGH: The cough is one simple, dry, barking cough, not wracking emphysemic spasms. Ellen McLaughlin's cough was a variation on a cat hacking up a furball. It was sharp, simple and effectively nonhuman.

FLYING: If you are mounting a production of the play, and you plan to have an airborne angel, which is a good thing, be warned: It's incredibly hard to make the flying work. Add a week to tech time.

Intermissions should be taken after Act Three and Act Four.

A NOTE ABOUT CUTTING: The final version of *Millennium Approaches* was edited more closely than *Perestroika* has been. The text can be performed as is, or in a shorter version made by eliminating one or all three of the following passages:

> Act Five Scene 5: In the Council of Continental Principalities. The entire introduction to the scene can be eliminated, and the scene can begin with the Angel of America saying "Most August Fellow Principalities, Angels Most High: I regret my absence at this session, I was detained." If this cut is made, the taped introduction should say "All Seven Myriad Infinite Aggregate Angelic Entities in Attendance, May Their Glorious Names Be Praised Forever and Ever, Hallelujah" instead of "Six of Seven, etc. . . ." and the scene should begin with Prior and the Angel of America standing in the midst of the Principalities, rather than entering after the scene begins.

Act Five Scenes 6 and 7 can be cut. Scene 7 can be played after Harper's final speech, before the Epilogue; if the scene is moved, Prior does *not* appear in it.

The elimination of these passages allows for a more stream-lined final act; I feel that some of the fun and complexity of the play is lost as a result. The decision should be made according to the specific circumstances of each production.

Because the soul is progressive,
it never quite repeats itself,
but in every act attempts the production
of a new and fairer whole.
                    —Ralph Waldo Emerson
                            "On Art"

ACT ONE:

Spooj

January 1986

Scene 1

In the darkness a Voice announces:

VOICE: In the Hall of Deputies, the Kremlin. January 1986. Aleksii Antedilluvianovich Prelapsarianov, the World's Oldest Living Bolshevik.

(Lights up on Prelapsarianov at a podium before a great red flag. He is unimaginably old and totally blind.)

ALEKSII ANTEDILLUVIANOVICH PRELAPSARIANOV: The Great Question before us is: Are we doomed? The Great Question before us is: Will the Past release us? The Great Question before us is: Can we Change? In Time? And we all desire that Change will come.
   (Little pause)
   (With sudden, violent passion) And *Theory?* How are we to proceed without *Theory?* What System of Thought

have these Reformers to present to this mad swirling planetary disorganization, to the Inevident Welter of fact, event, phenomenon, calamity? Do they have, as we did, a beautiful Theory, as bold, as Grand, as comprehensive a construct . . . ? You can't imagine, when we first read the Classic Texts, when in the dark vexed night of our ignorance and terror the seed-words sprouted and shoved incomprehension aside, when the incredible bloody vegetable struggle up and through into Red Blooming gave us Praxis, True Praxis, True Theory married to Actual Life. . . . You who live in this Sour Little Age cannot imagine the grandeur of the prospect we gazed upon: like standing atop the highest peak in the mighty Caucasus, and viewing in one all-knowing glance the mountainous, granite order of creation. You cannot imagine it. I weep for you.

And what have you to offer now, children of this Theory? What have you to offer in its place? Market Incentives? American Cheeseburgers? Watered-down Bukharinite stopgap makeshift Capitalism! NEPmen! Pygmy children of a gigantic race!

Change? Yes, we must must change, only show me the Theory, and I will be at the barricades, show me the book of the next Beautiful Theory, and I promise you these blind eyes will see again, just to read it, to devour that text. Show me the words that will reorder the world, or else keep silent.

If the snake sheds his skin before a new skin is ready, naked he will be in the world, prey to the forces of chaos. Without his skin he will be dismantled, lose coherence and die. Have you, my little serpents, a new skin?

(A tremendous tearing and crashing sound, the great red flag is flown out, and lights come up on the same tableau as at the close of Millennium Approaches: *Prior cowering in his bed, which is strewn with the wreckage of his bedroom ceiling; and the Angel, in a gown of surpassing whiteness, barefoot and magnificent, hovering in the air, facing him.)*

ALEKSII ANTEDILLUVIANOVICH PRELAPSARIANOV: Then we dare not, we *cannot*, we MUST NOT move ahead!

ANGEL:
> Greetings, Prophet!
> The Great Work Begins:
> The Messenger has arrived.

PRIOR: Go away.

Scene 2

The same night as at the end of Millennium, *late. Joe and Louis at Louis's new apartment in the arctic wastes of Alphabetland—barren of furniture, unpainted, messy, grim.*
> *Tense little pause. Louis, embarrassed, takes in the room.*

LOUIS: Alphabetland. This is where the Jews lived when they first arrived. And now, a hundred years later, the place to which their more seriously fucked-up grandchildren repair. *(Yiddish accent)* This is progress?
> It's a terrible mess.

JOE: It's a little dirty.

LOUIS: *Messy*, not dirty. That's an important distinction. It's dust, not dirt, chemical-slash-mineral, not organic, not like microbes, more like. . . . Can I take your tie off? *(He reaches towards Joe)*

JOE *(Stepping back)*: No, wait, I'm, um, um, uncomfortable, actually.

LOUIS: Me too, actually. Being uncomfortable turns me on.

JOE: Your, uh, boyfriend.

He's sick.

LOUIS: Very. He's not my boyfriend, we . . .

We can cap everything that leaks in latex, we can smear our bodies with nonoxynol-9, safe, chemical sex. Messy, but not dirty.

(Little pause)

Look I want to but I don't want to beg.

JOE: No, I . . .

LOUIS: Oh come on. *Please.*

JOE: I should go.

LOUIS: Fine! Ohblahdee, ohblahdah, life goes on. Rah.

JOE: What?

LOUIS: Hurry home to the missus.

(Pointing to Joe's left hand) Married gentlemen before cruising the Ramble should first remove their bands of gold.

Go if you're going. Go.

(Joe starts to leave. There is a moment at the door: Joe hesitating, Louis watching him. Joe goes to Louis, hugs him.)

JOE: I'm not staying.

LOUIS *(Sniffing)*: What kind of cologne is that?

JOE *(A beat, then)*: Fabergé.

LOUIS: OH! *Very* butch, very heterosexual high school. Fabergé.

(He gently breaks the hug, steps back)

LOUIS: You smell nice.

JOE: So do you.

LOUIS: Smell is . . . an incredibly complex and underappreci- ated physical phenomenon. Inextricably bound up with sex.

JOE: I . . . didn't know that.

LOUIS: It is. The nose is really a sexual organ.

Smelling. Is desiring. We have five senses, but only two that go beyond the boundaries . . . of ourselves. When you look at someone, it's just bouncing light, or when you hear them, it's just sound waves, vibrating air, or touch is just nerve endings tingling. Know what a smell is?

JOE: It's . . . some sort of. . . . No.

LOUIS: It's made of the molecules of what you're smelling. Some part of you, where you meet the air, is airborne.

(He goes up to Joe, close)

Little molecules of Joe . . . *(He inhales deeply)* Up my nose.

Mmmm. . . . Nice. Try it.

JOE: Try . . . ?

LOUIS: Inhale.

(Joe inhales.)

LOUIS: Nice?

JOE: Yes.

I . . .

LOUIS *(Quietly)*: Ssssshhhh.

Smelling. And tasting. First the nose, then the tongue.

JOE: I just don't . . .

LOUIS: They work as a team, see. The nose tells the body—the heart, the mind, the fingers, the cock—what it wants, and then the tongue explores, finding out what's edible, what isn't, what's most mineral, food for the blood, food for the bones, and therefore most delectable.

(He licks the side of Joe's cheek)
Salt.

(Louis kisses Joe, who holds back a moment and then responds.)

LOUIS: Mmm. Iron. Clay.

(Louis slips his hand down the front of Joe's pants. They embrace more tightly. Louis pulls his hand out, smells and tastes his fingers, and then holds them for Joe to smell.)

LOUIS: Chlorine. Copper. Earth.

(They kiss again.)

LOUIS: What does that taste like?
JOE: Um . . .
LOUIS: What?
JOE: Well. . . . Nighttime.
LOUIS: Stay?
JOE: Yes.
      (Still stalling) Louis?
LOUIS *(Unbuttoning Joe's shirt)*: Hmmm?
JOE: What did that mean, ohblahdee, oblah . . .
LOUIS: Sssssh. Words are the worst things. Breathe. Smell.
JOE: But . . .
LOUIS: Let's stop talking. Or if you have to talk, talk dirty.

Scene 3

Mr. Lies is sitting alone, playing the oboe, in Harper's imaginary Antarctica. Harper enters dragging a small pine tree which she has felled. The fantasy explorer gear is gone; she is dressed in the hastily assembled outfit in which she fled the apartment at the end of Act Two of Millenium; *she's been outdoors for three days now and looks it—filthy and disheveled.*

HARPER: I'm FREEZING! IT'S TOO COLD! What happened to global warming?

MR. LIES *(Stops playing; pointing to the tree)*: Where did you get that?

HARPER: Um. . . . From the . . . the great antarctic pine forests. Right over that hill.

MR. LIES: There are no pine forests in Antarctica.

HARPER: This one's a blue spruce.

MR. LIES: You keep messing with the idyllic, you're gonna wind up to your knees in slush.

HARPER: I chewed this pine tree down. With my teeth. Like a beaver. I'm *hungry*, I haven't eaten in three days! I'm going to use it to build . . . something, maybe a fire.

(Mr. Lies resumes his oboe-playing. For a moment, the magical antarctic light begins to dim, replaced by the glare of sodium park lights; the sea sounds and wind are drowned out by the sound of traffic as heard from the middle of a city park at night; Harper looks about, and as she does, Antarctica is restored a bit, though the city lights and sounds do not retreat entirely.)

MR. LIES: The oboe: official instrument of the International Order of Travel Agents. If the duck was a songbird it would sing like this. Nasal, desolate, the call of migratory things.

(Joe enters the scene, looking around, uncertain of where he is till he sees Harper. He has Louis's bedsheet wrapped around his waist.)

MR. LIES: The Eskimo is back.

HARPER: I know.

    I wanted a real Eskimo, one with sense enough to put on pants in sub-zero weather, not this, this is just . . .

JOE: Hey, buddy.

HARPER: I don't understand why I'm not dead. When your heart breaks, you should die.

    But there's still the rest of you. There's your breasts, and your genitals, and they're amazingly stupid, like babies or faithful dogs, they don't get it, they just want him. Want him.

JOE: I looked for you. I've been everywhere.

HARPER: Like that? It's indecent.

JOE: No, I. . . . I'm not looking now. I guess I'm having an adventure.

HARPER: Is it . . . fun?

JOE: Scary fun. Yes.

HARPER: Can I come with you? This isn't working anymore. I'm cold.

JOE: I wouldn't want you to see.

HARPER: Think it's worse than what I imagine? It's not.

JOE: I should go.

HARPER: Bastard. You fell out of love with me.

JOE: That isn't true, Harper.

HARPER: Then come back.

(Little pause.)

JOE: I can't.

(He vanishes. Mr. Lies plays the oboe—a brief, wild lament. The magic antarctic night is now completely gone. The ordinary sounds of the park and the city in the distance.)

MR. LIES: Blues for the death of heaven.

HARPER: If I was a good Mormon I could have pulled it off.

MR. LIES: You overreached. Tore a big old hole in the sky. No Eskimo in Antarctica.

HARPER: No. No trees either.

MR. LIES *(Pointing to the chewed-down pine tree)*: So where did you get that?

HARPER: From the Botanical Gardens Arboretum. It's right over there. Prospect Park. We're still in Brooklyn I guess.

(The lights of a police car begin to flash.)

MR. LIES *(Vanishing)*: The Law for real.

HARPER *(Raising her arms over her head)*: Busted. Damn. What a lousy vacation.

Scene 4

In the Pitt apartment in Brooklyn. A telephone rings. Hannah, carrying the bags she had with her and wearing the coat she had on in Act Three Scene 4 of Millennium, enters the apartment, drops the bags, runs for the phone.

HANNAH: Pitt residence.

No, he's out. No I have no idea where he is. I have no idea. I have no idea. No idea. No. No. This is his mother.

OH MY LORD! Is she. . . . You. . . . Wait, officer, I don't. . . . You found her in the. . . . Prospect Park? I don't. . . . She *what?* A pine tree? Why on earth would she chew a . . .

(Very severe) Well you have no business laughing about it, so you can stop that right now, that's ugly.

I don't know where that is, I just arrived from Salt Lake and I barely found Brooklyn. I'll take a . . . a taxi-cab. Well yes of course right now! *No.* No hospital. We don't need any of that. She's not insane, she's just . . . peculiar. Tell her to behave. Tell her . . . Mother Pitt is coming. *(She hangs up)*

Scene 5

Prior in bed, alone, asleep, later the same night. The room is intact, no trace of the demolished ceiling. He is having a nightmare. He wakes up.

PRIOR: OH! Oh.

(He looks under the covers. He discovers that the lap of his pajamas is soaked in cum)

Fuck fuck fuck.

Will you look at this! First goddamn orgasm in months and I slept through it.

(He picks up the telephone receiver, dials a number. The phone rings by Belize's workstation on the tenth floor of New York Hospital. Belize answers.)

BELIZE: Ten East.

PRIOR: I am drenched in spooj.

BELIZE: Spooj?

PRIOR: Cum. Jiz. Ejaculate.

BELIZE: Spooj?

PRIOR: Onomatapoetic, isn't it.

> I've had a wet dream.

BELIZE: Well about time. Miss Thing has been abstemious. She has stored up beaucoup de spooj.

PRIOR: It was a woman.

BELIZE: You turning straight on me?

PRIOR: Not a *conventional* woman.

BELIZE: Grace Jones?

(Little pause. Prior looks at the ceiling.)

BELIZE: Hello?

PRIOR: An angel.

BELIZE: Oh FABULOUS.

PRIOR: I feel . . . lascivious. Come over.

BELIZE: I spent the whole day with you, I *do* have a life of my own, you know.

PRIOR: I'm sad.

BELIZE: I thought you were lascivious.

PRIOR: Lascivious sad. Wonderful and horrible all at once, like . . . like there's a war inside. My eyes are funny, I . . . *(He touches his eyes)* Oh.

> I'm crying.

BELIZE: Prior?

PRIOR: I'm scared. And also full of, I don't know, Joy or something. Hope.

(In the hospital, Henry, Roy's doctor, enters.)

HENRY: Are you the duty nurse?

BELIZE: Yo.

> Look, baby, I have to go, I'll . . .

HENRY: Are you the duty nurse?

BELIZE *(To Henry)*: Yo, I said.

PRIOR: Sing something first. Sing with me.

HENRY: Why are you dressed like that?

BELIZE: You don't like it?

PRIOR: Just one little song. Some hymn.

HENRY: Nurses are supposed to wear white.

BELIZE: Doctors are supposed to be home, in Westchester, asleep.

> *(To Prior)* What hymn?

PRIOR: Ummm . . . "Hark the Herald Angels . . ."

HENRY: *Nurse.*

BELIZE: One moment, *please.* This is an emergency.

> *(To Prior, singing)*
> Hark the Herald Angels sing . . .

PRIOR *(Joining in)*:

> Glory to the newborn king.
> Peace on earth and mercy mild,
> God and sinners reconciled . . .

HENRY *(Over the song)*: What's your name?

(Belize sings louder.)

BELIZE AND PRIOR:

> JOYFUL all ye nations rise,
> Join the triumph of the skies!

With Angelic Hosts proclaim:
Christ is born in Bethlehem!
Hark the herald angels sing,
Glory to the newborn king!

BELIZE: Call you back. There's a man bothering me.

PRIOR: Je t'aime.

(Belize hangs up.)

BELIZE: Now may I help you doctor or are you just cruising me?

HENRY: Emergency admit, Room 1013. Here are the charts.
(He hands medical charts to Belize) Start the drip, Gamma
G and he'll need a CTM, radiation in the morning so
clear diet and . . .

BELIZE *(Reading the chart)*: "Liver cancer"? Oncology's on six,
doll.

HENRY: This is the right floor.

BELIZE: It says liver cancer.

HENRY *(Lashing out)*: I don't give a *fuck* what it *says. I* said this is
the right floor. Got it?

BELIZE: Ooooh, testy . . .

HENRY: He's a very important man.

BELIZE: Oh, OK. Then I *shouldn't* fuck up his medication?

HENRY: I'll be back in the morning.

BELIZE: Safe home.

(Henry leaves.)

BELIZE: Asshole.

(Belize picks up phone, dials; Prior answers.)

BELIZE: I have some piping hot dish.

PRIOR: How hot can it be at three in the . . . ?

BELIZE: Get out your oven mitts.

Guess who just checked in with the troubles?

The Killer Queen Herself. New York's number-one closeted queer.

PRIOR: *Koch?*

BELIZE: NO! Not Koch. *(He whispers into the receiver)*

PRIOR *(Shock, then)*: The Lord moves in mysterious ways.

BELIZE: Fetch me the hammer and the pointy stake, girl. I'm a-going in.

Scene 6

Roy in his hospital bed, sick and very scared. Belize enters with the IV drip.

ROY: Get outta here you, I got nothing to say to you . . .

BELIZE: Just doing my . . .

ROY: I want a white nurse. My constitutional right.

BELIZE: You're in a hospital, you don't have any constitutional rights.

(He begins preparing Roy's right arm for the IV drip, palpating the vein, disinfecting the skin, etc.)

ROY *(Getting nervous about the needle)*: Find the vein, you moron, don't start jabbing that goddamned spigot in my arm till you find the fucking vein or I'll sue you so bad they'll repossess your teeth you dim black motherf . . .

BELIZE *(Had enough; very fierce)*: Watch. Yourself.

You don't talk that way to me when I'm holding

something this sharp. Or I might slip and stick it in your heart. If you have a heart.

ROY: Oh I do. Tough little muscle. Never bleeds.

BELIZE: I'll bet.

Now I've been doing drips a long time. I can slip this in so easy you'll think you were born with it. Or I can make it feel like I just hooked you up to a bag of Liquid Drano. So you be nice to me or you're going to be one sorry asshole come morning.

ROY: Nice.

BELIZE: Nice and quiet.

(He puts the drip needle in Roy's arm)
There.

ROY *(Fierce)*: I *hurt*.

BELIZE: I'll get you a painkiller.

ROY: Will it knock me out?

BELIZE: I sure hope so.

ROY: Then shove it. Pain's . . . nothing, pain's life.

BELIZE: Sing it, baby.

ROY: When they did my facelifts, I made the anesthesiologist use a local. They lifted up my whole face like a dinner napkin and I was wide awake to see it.

BELIZE: Bullshit. No doctor would agree to do that.

ROY: I can get anyone to do anything I want. For instance: Let's be friends. *(Sings)* "We shall overcome . . . "

Jews and coloreds, historical liberal coalition, right? My people being the first to sell retail to your people, your people being the first people my people could afford to hire to sweep out the store Saturday mornings, and then we all held hands and rode the bus to Selma. Not me of course, I don't ride buses, I take cabs. But the thing about the American Negro is, he never went Communist. Loser

Jews did. But you people had Jesus so the reds never got to you. I admire that.

BELIZE: Your chart didn't mention that you're delusional.

ROY: Barking mad. Sit. Talk.

BELIZE: Mr. Cohn. I'd rather suck the pus out of an abscess. I'd rather drink a subway toilet. I'd rather chew off my tongue and spit it in your leathery face. So thanks for the offer of conversation, but I'd rather not.

(Belize starts to exit, turning off the light as he does.)

ROY: Oh forchristsake. Whatta I gotta do? Beg? I don't want to be alone.

(Belize stops.)

ROY: Oh how I fucking *hate* hospitals, *nurses*, this waste of time and . . . *wasting* and weakness, I want to kill the . . . Course they can't kill this, can they?

(Pause. Belize says nothing.)

ROY: No. It's too simple. It knows itself. It's harder to kill something if it knows what it is.

Like pubic lice. You ever have pubic lice?

BELIZE: That is none of your . . .

ROY: I got some kind of super crabs from some kid once, it took twenty drenchings of Kwell and finally shaving to get rid of the little bastards. *Nothing* could kill them. And every time I had to itch I'd smile, because I learned to respect them, these unkillable crabs, because . . . I learned to identify. You know? Determined lowlife. Like me.

You've seen lots of guys with this . . .

BELIZE *(Little pause, then)*: Lots.

ROY: How do I look, comparatively?

BELIZE: I'd say you're in trouble.

ROY: I'm going to die. Soon.

That was a question.

BELIZE: Probably. Probably so.

ROY: Hah.

I appreciate the . . . the honesty, or whatever . . .

If I live I could sue you for emotional distress, the whole hospital, but . . .

I'm not prejudiced, I'm not a prejudiced man.

(Pause. Belize just looks at him.)

ROY: These racist guys, simpletons, I never had any use for them—too rigid. You want to keep your eye on where the most powerful enemy really is. I save my hate for what counts.

BELIZE: Well. And I think that's a good idea, a good thing to do, probably.

(Little pause)

(With great effort and distaste) This didn't come from me and I *don't* like you but let me tell you a thing or two:

They have you down for radiation tomorrow for the sarcoma lesions, and you don't want to let them do that, because radiation will kill the T-cells and you don't have any you can afford to lose. So tell the doctor no thanks for the radiation. He won't want to listen. Persuade him.

Or he'll kill you.

ROY: You're just a fucking nurse. Why should I listen to you over my very qualified, very expensive WASP doctor?

BELIZE: He's not queer. I am. *(He winks at Roy)*

ROY: Don't wink at me.

> You said a thing or two. So that's one.

BELIZE: I don't know what strings you pulled to get in on the azidothymidine trials.

ROY: I have my little ways.

BELIZE: Uh-huh.

> Watch out for the double blind. They'll want you to sign something that says they can give you M&M's instead of the real drug. You'll die, but they'll get the kind of statistics they can publish in the *New England Journal of Medicine*. And you can't sue 'cause you signed. And if you don't sign, no pills.

> So if you have any strings left, pull them, because everyone's put through the double blind and with this, time's against you, you can't fuck around with placebos.

ROY: You hate me.

BELIZE: Yes.

ROY: Why are you telling me this?

BELIZE: I wish I knew.

(Pause.)

ROY *(Very nasty)*: You're a butterfingers spook faggot nurse. I think . . . you have little reason to want to help me.

BELIZE: Consider it solidarity. One faggot to another.

(Belize snaps his fingers, turns, exits. Roy calls after him.)

ROY: Any more of your lip, boy, and you'll be flipping Big Macs in East Hell before tomorrow night!
> *(A beat. He picks up his bedside phone)*
> And get me a real phone, with a hold button, I mean

look at this, it's just one little line, how am I supposed to perform basic bodily functions on *this*?

(He thinks a minute, picks up the receiver, clicks the hang-up button several times)

Yeah who is this, the operator? Give me an outside line. Well then dial for me. It's a medical emergency darling, dial the fucking number or I'll strangle myself with the phone cord. 202-733-8525.

(Little pause)

Martin Heller. Oh hi Martin. Yeah I know what time it is, I couldn't sleep, I'm busy dying. Listen Martin, this drug they got me on, azido-methatalo-molamoca-whatchamacallit. Yeah. AZT.

I want my own private stash, Martin. Of serious Honest-Abe medicine. That I control, here in the room with me. No placebos, I'm no good at tests, Martin, I'd rather cheat. So send me my pills with a get-well bouquet, *PRONTO*, or I'll ring up CBS and sing Mike Wallace a song: the ballad of adorable Ollie North and his secret contra slush fund.

(He holds the phone away from his ear; Martin is excited)

Oh you only *think* you know all I know. *I* don't even know what all I know. Half the time I just make it up, and it *still* turns out to be true! We learned that trick in the fifties. Tomorrow, you two-bit scumsucking shitheel flypaper insignificant dried-out little turd. A nice big box of drugs for Uncle Roy. Or there'll be seven different kinds of hell to pay. *(He slams the receiver down)*

Scene 7

The same night and then several nights after, over the course of three weeks. Split scene: Joe and Louis in bed in Alphabetland; Hannah and Harper in the Pitt apartment in Brooklyn. Hannah stands looking at Harper, who is dressed in a nightdress, picking her teeth.

HANNAH: It's late now, you should get into bed.

I can't believe you chewed down that tree.

HARPER: I thought I was a beaver. After that, the rest was easy.

HANNAH: Park trees are public property, Harper, you can't go around gnawing on . . .

HARPER *(Glares at her, then)*: This is Brooklyn, Mother Pitt. You live in Salt Lake. What are you doing here?

HANNAH: I sold my house.

(Harper turns around, goes back inside the bedroom, shutting the door.)

HANNAH: Can I get you some . . . tea, or . . . dental floss, or . . .

LOUIS: That was great. You were great. Was I? Great? Or good, even?

JOE: Sssshhh, no talk now, I just want to breathe.

LOUIS: OK.

(Tense little pause)

Why did you follow me tonight?

JOE *(A look at Louis, then)*: I'm . . . suspended.

Sort of remote from the earth. Like I've left no traces, like I haven't been here at all.

LOUIS: But . . .

JOE: Till tonight.

I was here. With you. This has consequence. This was new.

I keep expecting divine retribution for this, but . . . I'm . . . actually happy. Actually.

LOUIS: Are you. . . . What? Catholic, or . . .

JOE: Um, Protestant. Sort of.

LOUIS: I don't believe in God. I think you should know that before we fuck again. I used to believe but. . . . If there was a God He would've clobbered me by now. I'm the incontrovertible argument against the existence of a just God, or at least against His competence or attentiveness or . . .

JOE: Stop suffering.

LOUIS: I have no right not to suffer, if I failed to suffer the universe would become unbalanced.

(Joe bites one of Louis's nipples.)

(Hannah enters the apartment dressed for work at the Mormon Visitor's Center. Harper is slouched in a chair.)

HANNAH: I'm back.

LOUIS: Oh God, Oh God, I *believe*, I *believe*!

(Joe and Louis begin to fuck again.)

HANNAH: You haven't been out of that nightdress in two weeks now.

HARPER *(Dull, flat)*: I watched TV before you got home.

HANNAH: Well that's progress.

HARPER: It was a show about Antarctica. Female polar bears

were being chased by men in snowsuits. The men in snowsuits videotaped the polar bears running to escape. The bears went: *(She makes the deep wheezy hooting of a panicky animal)* and their tongues lolled and their eyes rolled in their stupid tiny heads and the men stabbed them in their huge butts with hypodermic needles, knocked them out. And then they shoved frozen polar bear sperm pencils up their cooters.

The bears looked like rugs. The men all looked like . . .

Good night.

HANNAH: There are no polar bears in Antarctica.

HARPER: THE ARCTIC THEN THE GODDAMNED ARCTIC WHAT THE FUCK DIFFERENCE DOES IT . . .

HANNAH: Profanity is *not* required.

Dress yourself and come with me to the Visitor's Center. Do some work.

HARPER: I don't want to work.

HANNAH: What do you want to do.

HARPER *(Bright smile)*: Die. *(She goes inside, slams the door)*

(Days pass. Joe and Louis, still in bed.)

JOE: You think happiness is about being totally happy.

HANNAH: Are you going to stay in bed forever?

JOE: Since you believe the world is perfectable you find it always unsatisfying. But you must reconcile yourself to its unperfectability by being thoroughly *in* the world but not *of* it.

LOUIS: Sounds like schizophrenia.

JOE: No, it's the end of a nineteenth-century socialist romanticist conflation of government and society, law and Justice, idea and action, irreconcilables which only meet at some remote horizon, like parallels converging in infinity. The rhythm of history is conservative. Change is geologically slow. You must accept that. And accept as rightfully yours the happiness that comes your way.

LOUIS: But that's only half the picture, that's the ego-anarchist-cowboys-shrilling-for-no-government part of the Republicans but what about the other half, the religious fanatics who want to control every breath every citizen takes? I mean you say law isn't Justice and Justice isn't morals but really, who if not the Right is putting the prude back in Jurisprudence?

JOE: No but see, there you go again! We're a movement, this is politics, not a representation of some pure force, it's. . . . Do you want to be pure, or do you want to be effective? Choose. Even if our methods seem . . . extreme, even. We've worked hard to build a movement.

LOUIS: But McCarthyism. Watergate.

(Joe kisses Louis.)

LOUIS: Pat Buchanan. Jesse Helms.
JOE: Barry Goldwater.

(They kiss.)

JOE: George Will.
LOUIS: George Bush.

(They kiss.)

LOUIS: Newt Gingrich. Objectively speaking, a rum bunch.
JOE: Responsible for everything bad and evil in the world.
LOUIS: Throw Reagan on the pile and you're not far off.

JOE: Oh if people like you didn't have President Reagan to demonize where would you be?

LOUIS: If he didn't have people like me to demonize where would *he* be? Upper-right-hand square on *The Hollywood Squares*.

This is interesting. I'm exploring my dark side these days, I'm losing myself in some ideological leather bar. The more appalling I find your politics the more I want to hump you. Bunker fucking; burn me up; may I never ever reemerge.

(Little pause.)

JOE: I don't want to be punishment for you.

LOUIS: What do you want to be?

JOE: Um. . . . A friend, I guess, a . . .

LOUIS: You are. Believe me. You protect me.
From all the buried and the unburied dead.
Let's spend the month in bed.

(They start to fuck.)

(A week passes. Harper stands in a bra and panties and stockings. Hannah, in a bathrobe, has a dress over her arm. A pair of shoes stands ready nearby.)

HANNAH: Did you wash up?

(Harper nods.)

HANNAH: Good.
Now let's slip this on.

(They put the dress on Harper.)

HANNAH: Good. It's pretty.
Shoes?

(Harper steps into them.)

HANNAH: Good. Now let's see about the hair.

(Harper bends over; Hannah combs Harper's hair.)

HANNAH: At first it can be very hard to accept how disappointing life is, Harper, because that's what it is and you have to accept it. With faith and time and hard work you reach a point . . . where the disappointment doesn't hurt as much, and then it gets actually easy to live with. Quite easy. Which is in its own way a disappointment. But. There.

HARPER *(Angry)*: I miss Joe's penis.

HANNAH: And I'm sure you'll understand it if I don't feel comfortable discussing that.

HARPER: It's five AM, Mother Pitt. I hate this dress.

HANNAH: I get there first. I open up.
I leave messages for him at his office. He leaves them for me. He won't come to the phone.
I'll fix myself now. And we can go. *(She exits)*

JOE: Freedom is where we bleed into one another. Right and Left. Freedom is the far horizon where lines converge. You will always have to make choices, and finally all life can offer you in the face of these terrible decisions is that you can make the choices freely. I did, I made a choice, I followed you. Louis. I came here. And this has taught me. . . . To be less afraid. Because the courage to choose enabled me to find you.

LOUIS: And our fucking brought you to this Republican epiphany?

JOE: Do you think I'm stupid?

LOUIS: No.

JOE: A liar.

LOUIS: No.

JOE: What you did when you walked out on him was hard to do. The world may not understand it or approve but it was *your* choice, what *you* needed, not some fantasy Louis but *you*. You did what you needed to do. And I consider you very brave.

LOUIS: Nobody does what I did, Joe. Nobody.

JOE: But maybe many want to. And maybe you should accept that you wanted to, and let him go for real. Forget your victimology. Forget that I am what I am and simply hear what I'm saying, free from politics and history: You are in yourself a good, good man. I admire you. I believe in you. I do.

LOUIS: I know you do.

       You seem to be able to live with what you've done, leaving your wife, you're not all torn up and guilty, you've . . . blossomed, but you're not a terrible person, you're a decent, caring man. And I don't know how that's possible, but looking at you it seems to be. You do seem free.

JOE: Yes.

LOUIS: And happy.

JOE: I am.

LOUIS: And at night you sleep peacefully. You don't have these terrible, terrible, awful, horrible dreams.

JOE: No. I never have any dreams at all.

(Little pause. Louis cries.)

JOE: Oh! Oh, you're. . . . Louis, Louis I . . .

(Joe takes Louis in his arms, cradles him.)

LOUIS: I'm . . . stressed.
No dreams at all. That would be amazing.
I'm OK.
JOE: I'm sorry if I . . .

(They kiss affectionately, romantically.)

LOUIS: It's dawn, we should . . .
(He lies down)
Make spoons.

(Joe complies.)

LOUIS: Sweet dreams. Or oblivion. Sweet, sweet oblivion.

(A few seconds pass.)

JOE *(Very softly)*: Louis?
Louis?
Louis?
I love you.

(Harper appears.)

HARPER: Don't worry, I'm not really here.
I have terrible powers. I see more than I want to see.
Maybe I'm a witch.

JOE: You're not.

HARPER: I could be a witch. Why not? I married a fairy.

JOE: Please, Harper, just go, I . . .

LOUIS *(Waking from a drowse)*: Joe . . . ?
　　　Are you OK?

JOE: Yeah, yeah, I. . . . I have a screwy stomach. It's nothing.

HARPER *(Simultaneously)*: Talk softer, you're keeping him awake.
　　　Why am I here? You called me.

JOE: I didn't . . .

HARPER: You called me. Leave me alone if you're so god-damned happy.

JOE: I didn't call you.

HARPER: *THEN WHY AM I HERE?*

(Pause. They look at each other.)

HARPER: To see you again. Any way I can.
　　　You're a liar. You do so have dreams. Bad ones.
　　　OH GOD I WISH YOU WERE. . . . No I don't.
　　　DEAD. Yes, I do.

LOUIS: Joe?

HARPER: You can't save him. You never saved anyone. Joe in love. Isn't it pathetic.

JOE: What?

HARPER: You're turning into me.

JOE: GO.

(She vanishes.)

LOUIS: What's . . .

JOE: Night chills. Nothing. I just can't sleep.

ACT TWO:

The Epistle

(For Sigrid Wurschmidt)

February 1986

Scene 1

Prior and Belize after the funeral of a mutual friend, a major New York City drag-and-style queen. They stand outside a dilapidated funeral parlor on the Lower East Side. Belize is in defiantly bright and beautiful clothing. Prior is dressed oddly: a great long black coat and a huge, fringed, matching scarf, draped to a hoodlike effect. His appearance is disconcerting, menacing and vaguely redolent of the Biblical.

[In all the scenes that follow in which Prior appears, this is his costume—he adds to and changes it slightly but it stays fundamentally corvine, ragged and eerie.]

Three weeks have passed since Act One.

PRIOR: It was tacky.
BELIZE: It was divine.

He was one of the Great Glitter Queens. He couldn't be buried like a *civilian*. Trailing sequins and incense he came into the world, trailing sequins and incense he departed it. And good for him!

PRIOR: I thought the twenty professional Sicilian mourners were a bit much.

(Little pause)

A great queen; big fucking deal. That ludicrous spectacle in there, just a parody of the funeral of someone who *really* counted. We don't; faggots; we're just a bad dream the real world is having, and the real world's waking up. And he's *dead*.

(Little pause.)

BELIZE: Lately sugar you have gotten very strange. Lighten up already.

PRIOR: Oh I *apologize*, it was only a for-God's-sake funeral, a cause for fucking *celebration*, sorry if I can't join in with the rest of you death-junkies, gloating about your survival in the face of that . . . of his ugly demise because unlike you I have nothing to gloat about. Never mind.

(Angry little pause.)

BELIZE: And you *look* like Morticia Addams.

PRIOR: Like the Wrath of God.

BELIZE: Yes.

PRIOR: That is the intended effect.

My eyes are fucked up.

BELIZE: Fucked up how?

PRIOR: Everything's . . . closing in. Weirdness on the periphery.

BELIZE: Since when?

PRIOR: For three weeks. Since that night. Since the night when . . . *(He stops himself)*

BELIZE: Well what does the eye doctor say?

PRIOR: I haven't been.

BELIZE: Oh for *God's sake*. Why?

PRIOR: I was improving. Before.

　　　Remember my wet dream.

BELIZE: The angel?

PRIOR: It wasn't a dream.

BELIZE: Course it was.

PRIOR: No. I don't think so.

　　　I'm a prophet.

BELIZE: Say what?

PRIOR: I've been given a prophecy. A book. Not a *physical* book, or there was one but they took it back, but somehow there's still this book. In me. A prophecy. It . . . really happened, I'm . . . almost completely sure of it.

　　　(He looks at Belize) Oh stop looking so . . .

BELIZE: You're scaring me.

PRIOR: It was after Louis left me. Every night I'd been having these horrible vivid dreams. And then . . .

(Little pause.)

BELIZE: Then . . . ?

PRIOR: And then She arrived.

Scene 2

The Angel and Prior in Prior's bedroom, three weeks earlier: the wrecked ceiling, Prior in the bed (he changes into his PJ's as he moves to it), the Angel in the air. Belize watches from the street.

ANGEL:

　　　Greetings, Prophet!

The Great Work Begins:
The Messenger has arrived.

PRIOR: Go away.

ANGEL:

Attend:

PRIOR: Oh God there's a thing in the air, a thing, a thing.

ANGEL:

I I I I
Am the Bird of America, the Bald Eagle,
Continental Principality,
LUMEN PHOSPHOR FLUOR CANDLE!
I unfold my leaves, Bright Steel,
In salutation open sharp before you:
PRIOR WALTER
Long-descended, well-prepared . . .

PRIOR: No, I'm not prepared, for anything, I have lots to do,
I . . .

ANGEL *(With a gust of music)*:

American Prophet tonight you become,
American Eye that pierceth Dark,
American Heart all Hot for Truth,
The True Great Vocalist, the Knowing Mind,
Tongue-of-the-Land, Seer-Head!

PRIOR: Oh, shoo! You're scaring the shit out me, get the fuck
out of my room. Please, oh please . . .

ANGEL:

Now:
Remove from their hiding place the Sacred Prophetic
Implements.

(Little pause.)

PRIOR: The *what*?

ANGEL:

> Remove from their hiding place the Sacred Prophetic Implements.
>
> *(Little pause)*
>
> Your dreams have revealed them to you.

PRIOR: What dreams?

ANGEL: You have had dreams revealing to you . . .

PRIOR: I haven't had a dream I can remember in months.

ANGEL: No . . . dreams, you. . . . Are you sure?

PRIOR: Yes. Well, the two dead Priors, they . . .

ANGEL: No not the heralds, not them. Other dreams. Implements, you must have. . . . One moment.

PRIOR: *This*, this is a dream, obviously, I'm sick and so I. . . . Well OK it's a pretty spectacular dream but still it's just some . . .

ANGEL: Quiet. Prophet. A moment, please, I. . . . The disorganization is . . . *(She coughs, looks up)* He says he hasn't had any . . . *(Coughs)*

> Yes.
>
> In the kitchen. Under the tiles under the sink.

PRIOR: You want me to . . . to tear up the kitchen floor?

ANGEL: Get a shovel or an axe or some . . . tool for dislodging tile and grout and unearth the Sacred Implements.

PRIOR: No fucking way! The ceiling's bad enough, I'll lose the lease, I'll lose my security deposit, I'll wake up the downstairs neighbors, their hysterical dog, I. . . . Do it yourself.

ANGEL *(A really terrifying voice)*: SUBMIT, SUBMIT TO THE WILL OF HEAVEN!

(An enormous gust of wind knocks Prior over. He glares at the Angel from the floor and shakes his head no. A standoff. The Angel coughs a little. There is a small, soft explosion in the kitchen offstage. A cloud of plaster dust drifts on.)

PRIOR: What did you. . . . What . . . ? *(Exits into the kitchen)*

ANGEL: And lo, the Prophet was led by his nightly dreams to the hiding place of the Sacred Implements, and. . . . Revision in the text: The Angel did help him to unearth them, for he was weak of body though not of will.

(Prior returns with a very dusty ancient leather suitcase.)

PRIOR: You cracked the refrigerator, you probably released a whole cloud of fluorocarbons, that's bad for the . . . the environment.

ANGEL: My wrath is as fearsome as my countenance is splendid. Open the suitcase.

(Prior does. He reaches inside and produces a pair of bronze spectacles with rocks instead of lenses.)

PRIOR: Oh, look at this. *(He puts them on)*
    Like, wow, man, totally Paleozoic. This is . . .
    (He stops suddenly. His head jerks up. He is seeing something)
    OH! OH GOD NO! OH . . . *(He tears off the spectacles)*
    That was terrible! I don't want to see that!

ANGEL: Remove the Book.

(Prior removes a large book with bright steel pages from the suitcase. There is a really glorious burst of music, more light, more wind.)

ANGEL:

    From the Council of Continental Principalities
    Met in this time of Crisis and Confusion:

Heaven here reaches down to disaster
And in touching you touches all of Earth.

(Music. She retrieves the spectacles, gives them to him.)

ANGEL:

Peep-stones.

(He cautiously puts them on.)

ANGEL:

Open me Prophet. I I I I am
The Book.
Read.

PRIOR: Wait. Wait. *(He takes off the glasses)*
How come. . . . How come I have this . . . um, erection? It's very hard to concentrate.

ANGEL: The stiffening of your penis is of no consequence.

PRIOR: Well maybe not to *you* but . . .

ANGEL:

READ!
You are Mere Flesh. I I I I am Utter Flesh,
Density of Desire, the Gravity of Skin:
What makes the Engine of Creation Run?
Not Physics But Ecstatics Makes The Engine Run:

(The Angel's lines are continuous through this section. Prior's lines overlap. They both get very *turned-on.)*

PRIOR *(Hit by a wave of intense sexual feeling)*: Hmmmm . . .

ANGEL:

The Pulse, the Pull, the Throb, the Ooze . . .

47

PRIOR: Wait, please, I. . . . Excuse me for just a minute, just a minute OK I . . .

ANGEL:

> Priapsis, Dilation, Engorgement, Flow:
> The Universe Aflame with Angelic Ejaculate . . .

PRIOR *(Losing control, he starts to hump the book)*: Oh shit . . .

ANGEL:

> The Heavens A-thrum to the Seraphic Rut,
> The Fiery Grapplings . . .

PRIOR: Oh God, I . . .

ANGEL:

> The Feathery Joinings of the Higher Orders,
> Infinite, Unceasing, The Blood-Pump of Creation!

PRIOR: OH! OH! I . . . OH! Oh! Oh, oh . . .

ANGEL *(Simultaneously)*: HOLY Estrus! HOLY Orifice! Ecstasis in Excelsis! AMEN!

(Pause. If they had cigarettes they'd smoke them now.)

PRIOR: Oh. Oh God.

ANGEL: The Body is the Garden of the Soul.

PRIOR: What *was* that?

ANGEL: Plasma Orgasmata.

PRIOR: Yeah well no doubt.

BELIZE: Whoa whoa whoa wait a minute excuse me please. You fucked this angel?

PRIOR: She fucked me. She has . . . well, she has eight vaginas.

ANGEL:

> REGINA VAGINA!
> Hermaphroditically Equipped as well with a Bouquet of Phallī . . .
> I I I I am Your Released Female Essence Ascendant.

PRIOR *(To Belize)*: The sexual politics of this are *very* confusing. God, for example is a man. Well, not a man, he's a flaming Hebrew letter, but a male flaming Hebrew letter.

ANGEL:
> The Aleph Glyph. Deus Erectus! Pater Omnipotens!

PRIOR: Angelic orgasm makes protomatter, which fuels the Engine of Creation. They used to copulate *ceaselessly* before . . .

> Each angel is an infinite aggregate myriad entity, they're basically incredibly powerful bureaucrats, they have no imagination, they can *do* anything but they can't invent, create, they're sort of fabulous and dull all at once:

ANGEL:
> Made for His Pleasure, We can only ADORE:
> Seeking something New . . .

PRIOR:
> God split the World in Two . . .

ANGEL:
> And made *YOU*:

PRIOR AND ANGEL:
> Human Beings:
> Uni-Genitaled: Female. Male.

ANGEL:
> In creating You, Our Father-Lover unleashed
> Sleeping Creation's Potential for Change.
> In YOU the Virus of TIME began!

PRIOR: In making us God apparently set in motion a potential in the design for change, for random event, for movement forward.

ANGEL:
> YOU *Think*. And You *IMAGINE*!
> Migrate, Explore, and when you do:

PRIOR: As the human race began to progress, travel, inter-
mingle, everything started to come unglued. Manifest
first as tremors in Heaven.

ANGEL:

    Heaven is a City Much Like San Francisco.

    House upon house depended from Hillside,

    From Crest down to Dockside,

    The green Mirroring Bay:

PRIOR: And there are earthquakes there, or rather, heaven-
quakes.

ANGEL:

    Oh Joyful in the Buckled Garden,

    Undulant Landscape Over Which

    The Threat of Seismic Catastrophe hangs:

    More beautiful because imperiled.

    POTENT: yet DORMANT: the Fault Lines of
        Creation!

BELIZE: So human progress . . .

PRIOR: Migration. Science. Forward Motion.

BELIZE: . . . shakes up Heaven.

ANGEL:

    Paradise itself Shivers and Splits,

    Each day when You awake, as though WE are only
        the Dream of YOU.

    PROGRESS! MOVEMENT!

    Shaking *HIM*:

BELIZE: God.

ANGEL:

    He began to leave us!

    Bored with His Angels, Bewitched by Humanity,

    In Mortifying Imitation of You, his least creation,

    He would sail off on Voyages, no knowing where.

    Quake follows quake,

Absence follows Absence:
Nasty Chastity and Disorganization:
Loss of Libido, Protomatter Shortfall:
We are his Functionaries; It is
BEYOND US:
Then:
April 18, 1906.
In That Day:

PRIOR: The Great San Francisco Earthquake. And also . . .

ANGEL:

In that day:

PRIOR *(Simultaneously)*: On April 18, 1906 . . .

ANGEL:

Our Lover of the Million Unutterable Names,
The Aleph Glyph from Which all Words Descend:
The King of the Universe:
HE Left

PRIOR: Abandoned.

ANGEL:

And did not return.
We do not know where HE has gone. HE may
never . . .
And bitter, cast-off, We wait, bewildered;
Our finest houses, our sweetest vineyards,
Made drear and barren, missing Him.
(Coughs)

BELIZE: Abandoned.

PRIOR: Yes.

BELIZE: I smell a motif. The man that got away.

PRIOR: Well it occurred to me. Louis.
Even now, if he came back I'd . . . *(He shrugs)*

BELIZE: Listen to your girlfriend.
I think the time has come to let him go.

PRIOR: That's not what the angels think, they think. . . . It's all gone too far, too much loss is what they think, we should stop somehow, go back.

BELIZE: But that's not how the world works, Prior. It only spins forward.

PRIOR: Yeah but forward into *what?*

ANGEL:

>Surely you see towards what We are Progressing:
>The fabric of the sky unravels:
>Angels hover, anxious fingers worry
>The tattered edge.
>Before the boiling of blood and the searing of skin
>Comes the Secret Catastrophe:
>Before Life on Earth becomes finally merely impossible,
>It will for a long time before have become completely unbearable.
>*(Coughs)*
>*YOU HAVE DRIVEN HIM AWAY!* YOU MUST STOP MOVING!

PRIOR *(Quiet, terrified)*: Stop moving.

ANGEL *(Softly)*:

>Forsake the Open Road:
>Neither Mix Nor Intermarry: Let Deep Roots Grow:
>If you do not MINGLE you will Cease to Progress:
>Seek Not to Fathom the World and its Delicate Particle Logic:
>You cannot Understand, You can only Destroy,
>You do not Advance, You only Trample.
>Poor blind Children, abandoned on the Earth,
>Groping terrified, misguided, over
>Fields of Slaughter, over bodies of the Slain:
>HOBBLE YOURSELVES!

There is No Zion Save Where You Are!

If you Cannot find your Heart's desire . . .

PRIOR: In your own backyard . . .

ANGEL, PRIOR AND BELIZE: You never lost it to begin with.

(The Angel coughs.)

ANGEL:

Turn back. Undo.

Till HE returns again.

PRIOR: Please. Please. Angel or dream, whatever you are . . .

BELIZE: It's a dream, baby . . .

PRIOR: Whatever you are, I don't understand this visitation, I don't understand what you want from me, I'm not a prophet, I'm a sick, lonely man, I . . .

What are you? Did you come here to save me or destroy me? Stop. Moving. That's what you want. Answer me! You want me dead.

(Pause. The Angel and Prior look at each other.)

ANGEL: YES. NO. NO.

(Coughs)

YES.

This is not in the Text, We *deviate* . . .

No more.

(She picks up the Book)

PRIOR: *I. WANT.* You to go away. I'm tired to death of being done to, walked out on, *infected,* fucked over and *now* tortured by some mixed-up, irresponsible angel, some. . . . Leave me alone.

(The Angel lands in front of Prior.)

53

ANGEL:

> You can't Outrun your Occupation, Jonah.
> Hiding from Me one place you will find me in
> another.
> I I I I stop down the road, waiting for you.

(She touches him, tenderly, and turns him, cradling him with one arm.)

ANGEL:

> You Know Me Prophet: Your battered heart,
> Bleeding Life in the Universe of Wounds.

(The Angel presses the volume against his chest. They both experience something unnameable—painful, joyful in equal measure. There is a terrifying sound. The Angel gently, lovingly lowers Prior to the ground.)

ANGEL:

> Vessel of the BOOK now: Oh Exemplum Paraly-
> ticum:
> On you in you in your blood we write have written:
> STASIS!
> The END.

(In gales of music, holding the Book aloft, the Angel ascends. The bedroom disappears. Prior stands, puts on his street clothes, and resumes his place beside Belize. They are back on the street in front of the funeral home.)

BELIZE: You have been spending too much time alone.
PRIOR: Not by choice. None of this by choice.

BELIZE: This is . . . worse than nuts, it's . . . well, don't migrate, don't mingle, that's . . . malevolent, some of us didn't exactly *choose* to migrate, know what I'm saying . . .

PRIOR *(Overlapping)*: I hardly think it's appropriate for you to get *offended*, I didn't invent this shit, it was *visited* on me . . .

BELIZE *(Overlapping on "offended")*: But it *is* offensive or at least monumentally confused and it's not . . . visited, Prior. By who? It *is* from you, what else is it?

PRIOR: Something else.

BELIZE: That's crazy.

PRIOR: Then I'm crazy.

BELIZE: No, you're . . .

PRIOR: Then it was an angel.

BELIZE: It was *not* an . . .

PRIOR: Then I'm crazy. The whole world is, why not me? It's 1986 and there's a *plague*, half my friends are dead and I'm only thirty-one, every goddamn morning I wake up and I think Louis is next to me in the bed and it takes me long minutes to remember . . . that this is *real*, it isn't just an impossible, terrible dream, so maybe yes I'm flipping out.

BELIZE *(Angry)*: You better not. You better fucking not flip out.

This is not dementia. And this is not real. This is just you, Prior, afraid of the future, afraid of time. Longing to go backwards so bad you made this angel up, a cosmic reactionary.

But there's no angel. You hear me?

For me? I can handle anything but not this happening to you.

PRIOR: Maybe I am a prophet. Not just me, all of us who are dying now. Maybe we've caught the virus of prophecy. Be still. Toil no more. Maybe the world has driven God from Heaven, incurred the angels' wrath.

ANGEL'S VOICE:

> Whisper into the ear of the World, Prophet,
> Wash up red in the tide of its dreams,
> And billow bloody words into the sky of sleep.

PRIOR: I believe I've seen the end of things. And having seen, I'm going blind, as prophets do. It makes a certain sense to me.

ANGEL'S VOICE:

> FOR THIS AGE OF ANOMIE: A NEW LAW!

PRIOR: And if I hate heaven my only resistance is to run.

ANGEL'S VOICE:

> Delivered this night, this silent night, from Heaven,
> Oh Prophet, to You.

ACT THREE:

Borborygmi
(The Squirming Facts Exceed the Squamous Mind)

February 1986

Scene 1

A week later. Roy in his hospital room. The pain in his gut is now constant and getting worse. He is on the phone, a more elaborate phone than in the previous scene. Legal documents and files are strewn on the bed. At the foot of the bed is a small, locked icebox.

ROY: No records no records what are you deaf I said I have no records for their shitty little committee, it's not how I work I . . .

(He has an incredibly bad abdominal spasm; he's in great pain. He holds the phone away, grimaces terribly, curls up into a ball and then uncurls, all the while making no sound.

Ethel appears in her hat and coat, walks to a chair by the bed and sits, watching Roy, silent. He watches her enter and then resumes his phone call, never taking his eyes off her.)

ROY: Those notes were lost. LOST. In a fire, water damage, I can't do this any . . .

(Belize enters with a pill tray.)

ROY *(To Belize)*: I threw up fifteen times today! I *COUNTED*.
    (Pause. To Ethel) What are *you* looking at?
    (To Belize) Fifteen times.
    (He goes back to the phone) Yeah?

BELIZE: Hang up the phone, I have to watch you take these . . .

ROY: The LIMO thing? Oh for the love of Christ I was acquitted twice for that, they're trying to kill me dead with this *harassment*, I have done things in my life but I never killed anyone.
    (To Ethel) Present company excepted. And you *deserved* it.
    (To Belize) Get the fuck outta here.
    (Back to the phone) Stall. It can't start tomorrow if we don't show, so don't show, I'll pay the old harridan back. I have to have a . . .

BELIZE: Put down the phone.

ROY: Suck my dick, Mother Teresa, this is life and death.

BELIZE: Put down the . . .

(Roy snatches the pill cup off the tray and throws the pills on the floor. Belize reaches for the phone. Roy slams down the receiver and snatches the phone away.)

ROY: You touch that phone and I'll bite. And I got rabies.
    And from now on, I supply my own pills. I already told 'em to push their jujubes to the losers down the hall.

BELIZE: Your own pills.

ROY: No double blind. A little bird warned me. The vultures . . .

(Another severe spasm. This time he makes noise) Jesus God these cramps, now I know why women go berserk once a. . . . AH FUCK!

(He has another spasm. Ethel laughs.)

ROY: Oh good I made her laugh.
(The pain is slightly less. He's a little calmer)
I don't trust this hospital. For all I know Lillian fucking *Hellman* is down in the basement switching the pills around—no, wait, she's dead, isn't she. Oh boy, memory, it's—. Hey Ethel, didn't Lillian die, did you see her up there, ugly, ugly broad, nose like a . . . like even a Jew should worry mit a punim like that. You seen somebody fitting that description up there in Red Heaven? Hah?

She won't talk to me. She thinks she's some sort of a deathwatch or something.
BELIZE: Who are you talking to?
ROY: I'm self-medicating.
BELIZE: With what?
ROY *(Trying to remember)*: Acid something.
BELIZE: Azidothymedine?
ROY: Gesundheit.

(Roy tosses a ring of keys to Belize.)

BELIZE: AZT? You got . . . ?
(He unlocks the icebox; it's full of bottles of pills)
ROY: One-hundred-proof elixir vitae.
Give me the keys.
BELIZE: You scored.
ROY: Impressively.

BELIZE: Lifetime supply.

There are maybe thirty people in the whole country who are getting this drug.

ROY: Now there are thirty-one.

BELIZE: There are a hundred thousand people who need it.

Look at you. The dragon atop the golden horde. It's not fair, is it?

ROY: No, but as Jimmy Carter said, neither is life. So put your brown eyes back in your goddam head, baby, I am not moved by an unequal distribution of goods on this earth. It's history, I didn't write it though I flatter myself I am a footnote. And you are a nurse, so minister and skedaddle.

BELIZE: If you live fifty more years you won't swallow all these pills.

(Pause)

I want some.

ROY: That's illegal.

BELIZE: Ten bottles.

ROY: I'm gonna report you.

BELIZE: There's a nursing shortage. I'm in a union. I'm real scared.

I have friends who need them. Bad.

ROY: Loyalty I admire. But no.

BELIZE *(Amazed, off guard)*: *Why?*

(Pause.)

ROY: Because you repulse me. *"WHY?"* You'll be begging for it next. *"WHY?"* Because I hate your guts, and your friends' guts, that's *why*. "Gimme!" So goddamned entitled. Such a shock when the bill comes due.

BELIZE: From what I read you never paid a fucking bill in your life.

ROY: *No one* has worked harder than me. To end up knocked flat in a . . .

BELIZE *(Overlapping)*: Yeah well things are tough all over.

ROY *(Continuous, over Belize)*: And you come *here* looking for *fairness*? *(To Ethel)* They couldn't *touch* me when I was alive, and now when I am dying they try this: *(He grabs up all the paperwork in two fists)* Now! When I'm a . . . *(Back to Belize)* That's fair? What am I? A dead man!

(A terrible spasm, quick and violent; he doubles up)

Fuck! What was I saying Oh God I can't remember any. . . . Oh yeah, dead.

I'm a goddam dead man.

BELIZE: You expect *pity*?

ROY *(A beat, then)*: I expect you to hand over those keys and move your nigger ass out of my room.

BELIZE: What did you say.

ROY: Move your nigger cunt spade faggot lackey ass out of my room.

BELIZE *(Overlapping, starting on "spade")*: Shit-for-brains filthy-mouthed selfish motherfucking cowardly cock-sucking cloven-hoofed pig.

ROY *(Overlapping)*: Mongrel. Dinge. Slave. Ape.

BELIZE: Kike.

ROY: *Now* you're talking!

BELIZE: Greedy kike.

ROY: Now you can have a bottle. But only one.

(Belize tosses the keys at Roy, hard. Roy catches them. Belize takes a bottle of the pills, then another, then a third, and leaves. As soon as he is out of the room Roy is wracked with a series of spasms; he's been holding them in.)

ROY: GOD I thought he'd never go!

(*To Ethel*) So what? Are you going to sit there all night?

ETHEL: Till morning.

ROY: Uh huh. The cock crows, you go back to the swamp.

ETHEL: No. I take the 7:05 to Yonkers.

ROY: What the fuck's in Yonkers?

ETHEL: The disbarment committee hearings. You been hocking about it all week. I'll have a look-see.

ROY: They won't let you in the front door. You're a convicted and executed traitor.

ETHEL: I'll walk through a wall.

(She starts to laugh. He joins her.)

ROY: Fucking SUCCUBUS! Fucking bloodsucking old bat!

(He picks up the phone, punches a couple of buttons and then puts the receiver back, dejectedly)

The worst thing about being sick in America, Ethel, is you are booted out of the parade. Americans have no use for sick. Look at Reagan: He's so healthy he's hardly human, he's a hundred if he's a day, he takes a slug in his chest and two days later he's out west riding ponies in his PJ's. I mean who does that? That's America. It's just no country for the infirm.

Scene 2

Later the same day. The Diorama Room of the Mormon Visitor's Center. The diorama is in a little proscenium theatre; the curtains are drawn shut. There are nice seats for the audience, and Harper is in one of them, dressed the same as in her last scene. She has bags of potato chips and M&M's and cans of soda scattered all around. Hannah enters with Prior.

HANNAH: This is the Diorama Room.
(*To Harper*) I thought we agreed that you weren't . . .
(*To Prior*) I'll go see if I can get it started.

(She exits. Prior sits. The lights in the room dim. A Voice on tape intones:)

VOICE: Welcome to the Mormon Visitor's Center Diorama Room. In a moment, our show will begin. We hope it will have a special message for you. Please refrain from smoking, and food and drink are not allowed. (*A chiming tone*) Welcome to the Mormon Visitor's . . .

(The tape lurches into very high speed, then smears into incomprehensibly low speed, then stops, mid-message, with an unpromising metallic blat.)

HARPER: They're having trouble with the machinery.
(She rips open a bag of nacho-flavored Doritos and offers them to Prior)
PRIOR: You're not supposed to eat in the . . .
HARPER: I can. I live here. Have we met before?
PRIOR: No, I don't . . . think so. You *live* here?
HARPER: There's a dummy family in the diorama, you'll see when the curtain opens. The main dummy, the big daddy dummy, looks like my husband, Joe. When they push the buttons he'll start to talk. You can't believe a word he says but the sound of him is reassuring. It's an *incredible* resemblance.
PRIOR: Are you a Mormon?

HARPER: Jack Mormon.

PRIOR: I beg your pardon?

HARPER: Jack Mormon. It means I'm flawed. Inferior Mormon product. Probably comes from jack rabbit, you know, I *ran*.

PRIOR: Do you believe in angels? In the Angel Mormon?

HARPER: Moroni, not Mormon, the Angel Moroni. Ask my mother-in-law, when you leave, the scary lady at the reception desk, if its name was Moroni why don't they call themselves Morons. It's from comments like that you can tell I'm jack Mormon. You're not a Mormon.

PRIOR: No, I . . .

HARPER: Just . . . distracted with grief.

PRIOR: I'm not. I was just walking and . . .

HARPER: We get a lot of distracted, grief-stricken people here. It's our specialty.

PRIOR: I'm not . . . distracted, I'm doing research.

HARPER: On Mormons?

PRIOR: On. . . . Angels. I'm a. . . . An Angelologist.

HARPER: I never met an angelologist before.

PRIOR: It's an obscure discipline.

HARPER: I can imagine. Angelology. The fieldwork must be rigorous. You'd have to drop dead before you saw your first specimen.

PRIOR: One. . . . I saw one. An angel. It crashed through my bedroom ceiling.

HARPER: Huh. That sort of thing always happens to me.

PRIOR: I have a fever. I should be in bed but I'm too anxious to lie in bed. You look *very* familiar.

HARPER: So do you.

But it's just not possible. I don't get out. I've only ever been here, or in some place a lot like this, alone, in the dark, waiting for the dummy.

(The lights in the Diorama Room darken; dramatic music; the curtains part and lights come up on the little stage where a classic wagon-train tableau is posed before a painted backdrop: a covered wagon and a Mormon family in the desert on the great trek from Missouri to Salt Lake. The family members are historically dressed mannequins: two sons, a mother and a daughter, and the father [who is actually the actor playing Joe]. The Voice on tape again:)

VOICE: In 1847, across fifteen hundred miles of frontier wilderness, braving mountain blizzards, desert storms, and renegade Indians, the first Mormon wagon trains made their difficult way towards the Kingdom of God.

HARPER: Want some nacho-flavored. . . . Hi Joe.

(The diorama comes to life. Sounds of a wagon train, the Largo from Dvorak's Ninth Symphony. The boy dummies, Caleb and Orrin, don't talk, you just hear their voices on a tape, and a pinspot hits their faces to indicate who is talking: the effect is unintentionally eerie. The father's face moves but not his body.)

CALEB *(Voice on tape)*: Father, I'm a-feard.

FATHER: Hush, Caleb.

ORRIN *(Voice on tape)*: The wilderness is so vast.

FATHER: Orrin, Caleb, hush. Be brave for your mother and your little sister.

CALEB: We'll try, Father, we want you to be proud of us. We want to be brave and strong like you.

HARPER *(Simultaneously)*: They don't have any lines, the sister and the mother. And only his face moves. That's not really fair.

ORRIN: When will we arrive in Zion, Father? When will our great exodus finally be done? All this wandering . . .

HARPER *(Overlapping on "Father")*: Never. You'll die of snake bite and your brother looks like scorpion food to me.

FATHER *(Overlapping on "scorpion")*: Soon boys, soon, just like the Prophet promised. The Lord leads the way.

CALEB: Will there be lots to eat there, Father?

HARPER *(On "Father")*: No, just sand.

CALEB *(Continuous)*: Will the desert flow with milk and honey? Will there be water there?

HARPER *(On "water")*: Oh, there's a big lake but it's salt, that's the joke . . .

FATHER *(On "joke")*: The Lord will provide for us, son, he always has.

ORRIN: Well, not *always* . . .

HARPER *(Continuous over above)*: . . . they drag you on your knees through hell and when you get there the water of course is undrinkable. Salt. It's a Promised Land, but what a disappointing promise!

FATHER *(On "promise")*: Sometimes He tests us, son, that's His way, but . . .

CALEB: Read to us, father, read us the story!

FATHER *(Chuckles)*: *Again?*

SONS: Yes! Yes! The Story! The Story! The story about the Prophet!

HARPER *(Simultaneously)*: The story! The story! The story about the Prophet!

FATHER: Well boys, well:

1823, the Prophet, who was a strapping lad, like everyone else in his time was seeking God, there were many churches, disputatious enough but who was Right? Could only be One True Church. All else darkness . . .

(Louis suddenly appears in the diorama.)

LOUIS: But how can a fundamentally theocratic religion exist in a pluralist democracy, I mean . . .

JOE: I'm busy, Louis.

LOUIS: But. . . . A *Mormon*? You're a . . . a . . . a . . .

JOE: Mormon. Yes.

LOUIS: But you . . . you *can't* be a Mormon! You're a lawyer! A *serious* lawyer!

PRIOR: Oh my God Oh my God.
    What. . . . What is going on here?

JOE *(Simultaneously)*: The chief clerk of the Chief Justice of the Supreme Court is . . .

HARPER: You know him?

PRIOR *(Closing his eyes)*: I'm delirious, I must be delirious.

LOUIS *(Looking around)*: God you should get a bigger office, it's crowded in . . .
    I don't like cults.

JOE: The Church of Jesus Christ of Latter Day Saints is not a cult.

LOUIS: Any religion that's not at least two thousand years old is a cult.

PRIOR: WHAT IS HE DOING IN THERE?

JOE *(Simultaneously)*: Oh shut up, Louis.

LOUIS: And I know people who would call *that* generous.

PRIOR: WHAT IS HE . . .

HARPER: Who? The little creep? He's in and out every day. I hate him. He's got absolutely *nothing* to do with the story.

PRIOR: Can you turn it off? The. . . . I'm leaving, I can't . . .

LOUIS: Why didn't you tell me that you . . .

JOE: It's a surprise?

LOUIS: No, no most of the men I go to bed with turn out to be

YEAH OF COURSE it's a surprise! I thought you were all out west somewhere with the salt flats and the cactuses. There's some sort of profound displacement going on here, I . . .

PRIOR: Louis.

LOUIS *(Hearing him)*: Did you. . .

JOE: What?

LOUIS: I thought I heard. . . . Somebody. Prior.
(To Joe) We have to talk.

JOE: I'm working.

LOUIS: Fuck it. This is a crisis. Now.

(Louis exits. Joe sighs and then follows.)

HARPER: Well the dummy never *left* with the little creep, he never left before. When they come in and they see he's gone, they'll blame me.

(Harper goes to the diorama stage and pulls its bright red curtain closed. She turns back and sees that Prior is crying.)

HARPER: You shouldn't do that in here, this isn't a place for real feelings, this is just storytime here, stop.

PRIOR: I never imagined losing my mind was going to be such hard work.

HARPER: Oh, it is.
Find someplace else to be miserable in. This is *my* place and I don't want you to do that here!

PRIOR: I JUST SAW MY LOVER, MY . . . ex-lover, with a . . . with your husband, with that . . . window-display Ken doll, in that . . . *thing*, I saw him, I . . .

HARPER: Well don't have a hissy fit, I told you it wasn't working right, it's just . . . the magic of the theatre or something.

Listen, if you see the creep, tell him to bring Joe . . . to bring the mannequin back, they'll evict me and this is it, it's nothing but it's the last place on earth for me. I can't go sit in Brooklyn.

(Hannah enters.)

HANNAH: What's all the . . .
 (She sees Prior crying. She glares at Harper)
 What did you do to him?
HARPER: Nothing! He just can't *adjust*, is all, he just . . .

(Hannah has gone to the diorama. She yanks the curtain open.)

HARPER: NO WAIT. Don't . . .

(The father dummy is back—a real dummy this time.)

HARPER: Oh. *(To Prior)* Look, we . . . imagined it.
HANNAH: This is a favor, they let me work here as a favor, but you keep making scenes, and look at this mess, it's a garbage scow!
HARPER *(Over Hannah, to Prior)*: It doesn't look so much like him, now. He's changed. Again.
HANNAH *(Overlapping)*: Are you just going to sit here forever, trash piling higher, day after day till. . . . Well till what?
HARPER *(Overlapping)*: You sound just like him. You even grind your teeth in your sleep like him.
HANNAH *(Overlapping)*: If I could get him to come back I would go back to Salt Lake tomorrow but I know my duty when I see it, and if you and Joe could say the same we . . .
HARPER *(Overlapping on "tomorrow")*: You can't go back to Salt

Lake, you sold your house! *(To Prior)* My mother-in-law! She sold her house! Her son calls and tells her he's a homo and what does she do? She sells her house! And she calls *me* crazy! *(To Hannah)* You have less of a place in this world than I do if that's possible.

PRIOR: Am I dreaming this, I don't understand.

HARPER: He saw an angel.

HANNAH: That's his business.

HARPER: He's an angelologist.

PRIOR: Well don't go blabbing about it.

HANNAH: If you aren't serious you shouldn't come in here.

HARPER *(Simultaneously)*: Either that or he's nuts.

PRIOR: It's a visitor's center; I'm visiting.

HARPER: He has a point.

HANNAH *(To Harper)*: Quiet!

(To Prior) It's for serious visitors, it's a serious religion.

PRIOR: Do they like, *pay* you to do this?

HARPER: She volunteers.

PRIOR: Because you're not very hospitable. I did see an angel.

HANNAH: And what do you want me to do about it? I have problems of my own.

The diorama's closed for repairs. You have to leave.
(To Harper) Clean up this mess. *(Exits)*

(Embarrassed little pause, then:)

HARPER *(Pointing to the Mormon Mother)*: His wife. His mute wife. I'm waiting for her to speak. Bet her story's not so jolly.

PRIOR: Imagination is a dangerous thing.

HARPER *(Looking at the father dummy)*: In certain circumstances, fatal. It can blow up in your face. If it turns out to be true. Threshold . . .

PRIOR AND HARPER: . . . of revelation.

(They look at each other.)

PRIOR: It's crazy time. I feel . . . this is nuts. I feel . . . this is nuts. We've never met, but I feel you know me incredibly well.

HARPER: Crazy time. The barn door's open now, and all the cows have fled.

You don't look well. You really should be home in bed.

PRIOR: I'll die there.

HARPER: Better in bed than on the street. Just ask anyone.

Till we meet again.

(Prior leaves. Harper sits alone.)

HARPER: Bitter lady of the Plains, talk to me. Tell me what to do.

(The Mormon Mother turns to Harper, then stands and leaves the diorama stage. She gestures with her head for Harper to follow her.)

HARPER: I'm stuck. My heart's an anchor.

MORMON MOTHER: Leave it, then. Can't carry no extra weight.

(The Mormon Mother steps out of the diorama, crosses to where Harper is sitting. Harper sits a moment. She goes to the diorama, gets in the Mormon Mother's seat.)

HARPER *(To the dummy father)*: Look at us. So perfect in place. The desert the mountains the previous century. Maybe I could have believed in you then. Maybe we should never have moved east.

MORMON MOTHER: Come on.

(They exit.)

Scene 3

Late that afternoon. Joe and Louis sitting shoulder to shoulder in the dunes at Jones Beach, facing the ocean. It's cold. The sound of waves and gulls and distant Belt Parkway traffic. New York Romantic. Joe is very cold, Louis as always is oblivious to the weather.

JOE: Louis . . . ?

LOUIS: The winter Atlantic. Wow, huh?

JOE: Ferocious. It's freezing, what are we . . .

LOUIS: There used to be guys in the dunes even when it snowed. Nothing deterred us from the task at hand.

JOE: Which was?

LOUIS: Exploration. Across an unmapped terrain. The body of the homosexual human male. Here, or the Ramble, or the scrub pines on Fire Island, or the St. Mark's Baths. Hardy pioneers. Like your ancestors.

JOE: Not exactly.

LOUIS: And many have perished on the trail.

I fucked around a whole lot more than he did. So why is he the sick one? No justice. Anyway I wanted you to see this.

JOE: Why?

LOUIS: No reason.

(Little pause.)

JOE: I love you.

LOUIS: No you don't.

JOE: Yes I do.

LOUIS: NO YOU DON'T. You think you do but that's just the gay virgin thing, that's . . .

JOE *(Tousling Louis's hair)*: Stop working so hard.

Listen to the ocean.

I love it when you can get to places and see what it used to be. The whole country was like this once. A paradise.

LOUIS: Ruined now.

JOE: It's a great country. Best place on earth. Best place to be.

LOUIS: I can't believe you're a Mormon. You never told me.

JOE: You never asked.

LOUIS: You said you were a Protestant.

JOE: I am. Sort of.

LOUIS: So what else haven't you told me?

So the fruity underwear you wear, that's . . .

JOE: A temple garment.

LOUIS: Oh my god. What's it for?

JOE: Protection. A second skin. I can stop wearing it if you . . .

LOUIS: How can you stop wearing it if it's a skin? Your past, your beliefs, your . . .

JOE: I'm not your enemy. Louis.

I do. . . . I am in love with you.

You and I, fundamentally, we're the same. We both want the same things.

LOUIS: I want to see Prior again.

(Joe stands up, moves away.)

LOUIS: I miss him, I . . .

JOE: You want to go back to . . .

LOUIS: I just. . . . Need to see him again.

>*(Little pause)*

>Don't you. . . . You must want to see your wife.

JOE: I do see her. All the time. *(Pointing to his head)* In here. I miss her, I feel bad for her, I. . . . I'm afraid of her.

LOUIS: Yes.

JOE: And I want more to be with . . .

LOUIS: I have to. See him. It's like a bubble rising up through rock, it's taken time, I don't know, the month in bed and the . . .

>Love is still what I don't get, it . . . never seems to fit into any of the schematics, wherever I'm going and whatever I've prepared for I always seem to have forgotten about love.

>I only know. . . . It's an unsafe thing. To talk about love, Joe.

>Please don't look so sad.

>I just. I have to see him again. Do you understand what I . . .

JOE: You don't want to see me anymore.

>Louis.

>Anything. Whatever you want. I can give up anything. My skin.

(He starts to remove his clothes. Louis, when he realizes what Joe is doing, tries to stop him.)

LOUIS: What are you doing, someone will see us, it's not a nude beach, it's freezing!

(Joe is half in, half out of his clothes. He has pulled the upper part of the garment off.)

JOE: I'm flayed.

> No past now. I could give up anything. Maybe . . . in what we've been doing, maybe I'm even infected.

LOUIS: No you're . . .

JOE: I don't want to be. I want to live now. And I can be anything I need to be. And I want to be with you.

(Louis starts to dress Joe.)

JOE *(As he's being dressed)*: You have a good heart and you think the good thing is to be guilty and kind always but it's not always kind to be gentle and soft, there's a genuine violence softness and weakness visit on people. Sometimes self-interested is the most generous thing you can be.

> You ought to think about that.

LOUIS: I will. Think about it.

JOE: You ought to think about . . . what you're doing to me. No, I mean. . . . What you need. Think about what you need. Be brave.

> And then you'll come back to me.

Scene 4

Night of the same day. Louis and Joe remain onstage from the previous scene.

> *Roy's hospital room. Roy is asleep. Belize enters, carrying a tray and a glass of water. He wakes Roy up.*

BELIZE: Time to take your pills.

ROY *(Waking)*: What? What time of . . .
>Water.

(Belize gives him a glass of water.)

ROY: Bitter.
>*Look* out there. Black midnight.
BELIZE: You want anything?
ROY: Nothing that comes from there. As far as I'm concerned
>you can take all that away.
>*(Seeing Belize)* Oh . . .
BELIZE: What?
ROY: Oh. The bogeyman is here.
>Lookit. A schvartze toytenmann.
>Come in, sweetheart, what took you so long?
BELIZE: You're flying, Roy. It's the morphine. They put mor-
>phine in the drip to stop the. . . . You awake? Can you see
>who I am?
ROY: Oh yeah, you came for my mama, years ago.
>You wrap your arms around me now. Squeeze the
>bloody life from me. OK?
BELIZE: Uh, no, it's not OK. You're stoned, Roy.
ROY: Dark strong arms, take me like that. Deep and sincere but
>not too rough, just open me up to the end of me.
BELIZE: Who am I, Roy?
ROY: The Negro night nurse, my negation.
>You've come to escort me to the underworld.
>*(A serious sexual invitation)* Come on.
BELIZE: You want me in your bed, Roy? You want me to take
>you away.
ROY: I'm ready . . .
BELIZE: I'll be coming for you soon. Everything I want is in the
>end of you.

ROY: So *now*. *God*, I'm ready.

Fucking slow like every black man.

Let me ask you something, sir.

BELIZE: *Sir?*

ROY: What's it like? After?

BELIZE: After . . . ?

ROY: This misery ends.

BELIZE: Hell or Heaven?

(Roy stares at Belize.)

BELIZE: Like San Francisco.

ROY: A city. Good. I was worried . . . it'd be a garden. I hate that shit.

BELIZE: Mmmm.

Big city, overgrown with weeds, but flowering weeds. On every corner a wrecking crew and something new and crooked going up catty-corner to that. Windows missing in every edifice like broken teeth, fierce gusts of gritty wind, and a gray high sky full of ravens.

ROY: Isaiah.

BELIZE: Prophet birds, Roy.

Piles of trash, but lapidary like rubies and obsidian, and diamond-colored cowspit streamers in the wind. And voting booths.

ROY: And a dragon atop a golden horde.

BELIZE: And everyone in Balenciaga gowns with red corsages, and big dance palaces full of music and lights and racial impurity and gender confusion.

(Roy laughs softly, delighted.)

BELIZE: And all the deities are creole, mulatto, brown as the mouths of rivers.

(Roy laughs again.)

BELIZE: Race, taste and history finally overcome.
And you ain't there.
ROY *(Happily shaking his head "no" in agreement)*: And
Heaven?
BELIZE: That *was* Heaven, Roy.
ROY: The fuck it was.
(Suspicious, frightened) Who are you?

(Little pause.)

BELIZE *(Whispering)*: I work for the KGB.
ROY: You and Paul Robeson.
(Trying to get his head clear) Do I know you.
BELIZE: Your negation.
ROY: Yeah. I know you. Nothing. A stomach grumble that
wakes you in the night. A dark place created in the
absence of me.

(Ethel enters.)

BELIZE: Been nice talking to you. Go to sleep now, baby. I'm
just the shadow on your grave.

Scene 5

*Harper and the Mormon Mother. Night. At the Brooklyn
Heights Promenade. Everyone from the previous two scenes
remains onstage.*

HARPER: It's not safe to be out on the street here, there are crazy people around.

MORMON MOTHER *(Looking at the skyline)*: Towers filled with fire. It's the Great Beyond.

HARPER: Manhattan.

Was it a hard thing, crossing the prairies?

MORMON MOTHER: You ain't stupid. So don't ask stupid. Ask something for real.

HARPER *(A beat, then)*: In your experience of the world. How do people change?

MORMON MOTHER: Well it has something to do with God so it's not very nice.

God splits the skin with a jagged thumbnail from throat to belly and then plunges a huge filthy hand in, he grabs hold of your bloody tubes and they slip to evade his grasp but he squeezes hard, he *insists*, he pulls and pulls till all your innards are yanked out and the pain! We can't even talk about that. And then he stuffs them back, dirty, tangled and torn. It's up to you to do the stitching.

HARPER: And then get up. And walk around.

MORMON MOTHER: Just mangled guts pretending.

HARPER: That's how people change.

(Prior appears. He's at home, slowly unwrapping his layers of black prophet clothes. He is very sick and sad.)

MORMON MOTHER: I smell a salt wind.

HARPER: From the ocean.

MORMON MOTHER: Means he's coming back. Then you'll know. Then you'll eat fire.

(Singing)

Bring back, bring back,
Oh bring back my bonnie to me, to me . . .
HARPER *(Joining in)*:
Bring back, bring back,
Oh bring back my bonnie to me.

(As they sing, Louis leaves Joe alone at the beach. Back in Manhattan, he goes to a street-side payphone, dials a number. Prior is alone in his bedroom. He is taking his medication. The phone rings in his apartment. He picks it up.)

PRIOR: Wait, I have a mouthful of pills and water, I . . .
LOUIS: Prior? It's Lou.

(Prior swallows.)

LOUIS: I want to see you.

ACT FOUR:

John Brown's Body

February 1986

Scene 1

A day later. Split scene: Louis sitting, cold, on a park bench; Roy and Joe in Roy's hospital room. Roy's in bed, hooked up as usual to an IV drip. His condition has worsened. Joe sits in a chair nearby.

ROY: If you want the smoke and puffery you can listen to Kissinger and Schultz and those guys, but if you want to look at the heart of modern conservatism, you look at me. Everyone else has abandoned the struggle, everything nowadays is just sipping tea with Nixon and Mao. That was *disgusting*, did you see that? Were you born yet?

JOE: Of course I . . .

ROY: My generation, we had *clarity*. Unafraid to look deep into the miasma at the heart of the world, what a pit, what a nightmare is there—*I* have looked, I have searched all my life for absolute bottom, and I found it, *believe* me: *Stygian*. How tragic, how brutal and short life is. How sinful people are. The immutable heart of what we are that bleeds through whatever we might become. All else is vanity.

I don't know the world anymore.

(He coughs)

After I die they'll say it was for the money and the headlines. But it was never the money: it's the moxie that counts. I never wavered. You: remember.

JOE: I will, Roy.

I was afraid you wouldn't want to see me. If you'd forgive me. For letting you down.

ROY: Forgiveness.

You seen a lady around here, dumpy lady, stupid . . . hat? She. . . . Oh boy. Oh boy, no she's off watching the hearings. Treacherous bitch.

JOE: Who?

ROY: Did you get a blessing from your father before he died?

JOE: A blessing?

ROY: Yeah.

JOE: No.

ROY: He should have done that. Life. That's what they're supposed to bless. Life.

(Roy motions for Joe to come over, then for him to kneel. He puts his hand on Joe's forehead. Joe leans the weight of his head into Roy's hand. They both close their eyes and enjoy it for a moment.)

JOE *(Quietly)*: Roy, I . . . I need to talk to you about . . .

ROY: Ssshah. Schmendrick. Don't fuck up the magic.

(He removes his hand) A *Brokhe*. You don't even have to trick it out of me, like what's-his-name in the Bible.

JOE: Jacob.

ROY: That's the one. A ruthless motherfucker, some bald runt, but he laid hold of his birthright with his claws and his teeth. Jacob's father—what was the guy's name?

JOE: Isaac.

ROY: Yeah. The sacrifice. That jerk.

My mother read me those stories.

See this scar on my nose? When I was three months old, there was a bony spur, she made them operate, shave it off. They said I was too young for surgery, I'd outgrow it but she insisted. I figure she wanted to toughen me up. And it worked.

I am tough. It's taking a lot . . . to dismantle me.

(Prior enters and sits on the bench, as far as he can from Louis.)

PRIOR: Oh this is going to be so much worse than I'd imagined.

LOUIS: Hello.

PRIOR: Fuck you you little shitbag.

LOUIS: Don't waste energy beating up on me, OK? I'm already taking care of that.

PRIOR: Don't see any bruises.

LOUIS: Inside.

PRIOR: You are one noble guy. Inside. Don't flatter yourself, Louis.

So. It's your tea party. Talk.

LOUIS: It's good to see you again. I missed you.

PRIOR: Talk.

LOUIS: I want to . . . try to make up.

PRIOR: Make up.

LOUIS: Yes. But . . .

PRIOR: Aha. But.

LOUIS: But you don't have to be so hostile. Don't I get any

points for trying to arrive at a resolution? Maybe what I
did isn't forgivable but . . .

PRIOR: It isn't.

LOUIS: But. I'm trying to be responsible. Prior. There are limits.
Boundaries. And you have to be reasonable.

Why are you dressed like that?

(Little pause.)

PRIOR: You were saying something about being reasonable.

LOUIS: I've been giving this a lot of thought. Yes I fucked up,
that's obvious. But maybe you fucked up too. You never
trusted me, you never gave me a chance to find my
footing, not really, you were so quick to attack and . . . I
think, maybe just too much of a victim, finally. Passive.
Dependent. And what I think is that people do have a
choice about how they handle . . .

PRIOR: You want to come back. Why?

LOUIS: I didn't say I wanted to . . .

(Pause.)

PRIOR: Oh.

No, you didn't.

LOUIS *(Softly, almost pleading)*: I can't. Move in again, start all
over again. I don't think it'd be any different.

(Little pause.)

PRIOR: You're seeing someone else.

LOUIS *(Shocked)*: What? No.

PRIOR: You are.

LOUIS: I'M NOT. Well, occasionally a . . . he's a . . . just a pickup, how do you . . .

PRIOR: Threshold of revelation. Now: Ask me how I know he's a Mormon.

(Pause. Louis stares.)

PRIOR: *Is* he a Mormon?
(Little pause)
Well, goddamn. Ask me how I knew.

LOUIS: How?

PRIOR: Fuck you. I'm a prophet.
(Furious) Reasonable? Limits? Tell it to my *lungs*, stupid, tell it to my lesions, tell it to the cotton-woolly patches in my eyes!

LOUIS: Prior, I . . . haven't seen him for days now . . .

PRIOR: I'm going, I have limits too.

(Prior starts to leave. He has an attack of some sort of respiratory trouble. He sits heavily on the bench. Louis starts to go near him, Prior waves him away. Prior looks at Louis.)

PRIOR: You cry, but you endanger nothing in yourself. It's like the idea of crying when you do it.
Or the idea of love.

ROY: Now you have to go.

JOE: I left my wife.
(Little pause)
I needed to tell you.

ROY: It happens.

JOE: I've been staying with someone. Else. For a whole month now.

ROY: It happens.
JOE: With a . . . man.

(Pause.)

ROY: A man?
JOE: Yes.
ROY: You're with a man?
JOE: Yes I . . .

(Roy sits up in his bed. He puts his legs over the side, away from where Joe is sitting.)

ROY: I gotta . . .
JOE: You . . . what, the . . . um, bathroom or . . .

(Roy stands, unsteadily. He starts to walk away from the bed. The IV tube in his arm extends to its full length and then pulls. Roy looks down at it, remembering it's there. In a calm, even disinterested manner he pulls it out of his arm.)

ROY: Ow.
JOE: Roy, what are you . . .

(Joe starts for the door, Roy stands still watching dark blood run down his arm.)

JOE (Calling off): Um, help, please, I think he . . .

(Belize enters with the portable oxygen, and then sees Roy.)

BELIZE: Holy shit. (He puts on rubber gloves, starts towards Roy)
ROY: Get the fuck away from me.

JOE *(Going towards Roy)*: Roy, please, get back into . . .

ROY: SHUT UP!

Now you listen to me.

(Joe nods.)

BELIZE: Get your . . .

ROY: SHUT UP I SAID.

(To Joe) I want you home. With your wife. Whatever else you got going, cut it dead.

JOE: I can't, Roy, I need to be with . . .

(Roy grabs Joe by the shirt, smearing it with blood.)

ROY: YOU NEED? Listen to me. Do what I say. Or you will regret it.

And don't talk to me about it. *Ever again.*

(Belize moves in, takes Roy to the bed and starts bandaging the puncture.)

ROY: I . . . never saw that coming. You kill me.

BELIZE *(To Joe)*: Get somewhere you can take off that shirt and throw it out, and don't touch the blood.

JOE: Why? I don't unders . . .

ROY: OUT! OUT! You already got my blessing—WHAT MORE DO YOU WANT FROM ME?

(He has a terrible wracking spasm)

BELIZE *(To Joe)*: Get the fuck outta here.

JOE: I . . . Roy, please I . . .

ROY *(Exhausted)*: You what, you want to stay and watch *this*? Well fuck you too.

(Joe leaves. Belize finishes bandaging.)

PRIOR: So. Your new lover.

LOUIS: He's not my . . .

PRIOR: Tell me where you met him.

LOUIS: In the park. Well, first at work, he . . .

PRIOR: He's a lawyer or a judge?

LOUIS: Lawyer.

PRIOR: A Gay Mormon Lawyer.

LOUIS: Yes. Republican too.

PRIOR: A Gay Mormon Republican Lawyer. *(With contempt)* Louis . . .

LOUIS: But he's sort of, I don't know if the word would be . . . well, in a way sensitive, and I . . .

PRIOR: Ah. A *sensitive* gay Republican.

LOUIS: He's just company. Companionship.

(Pause.)

PRIOR: Companionship. Oh.

You know just when I think he couldn't possibly say anything to make it worse, he does. Companionship. How *good*. I wouldn't want you to be *lonely*.

There are thousands of gay men in New York City with AIDS and nearly every one of them is being taken care of by . . . a friend or by . . . a lover who has stuck by them through things worse than my. . . . So far. Everyone got that, except me. I got you. Why? What's wrong with me?

(Louis is crying.)

PRIOR: Louis?

Are you really bruised inside?

LOUIS: I can't have this talk anymore.

PRIOR: Oh the list of things you can't do. So fragile! Answer me: Inside: Bruises?

LOUIS: Yes.

PRIOR: Come back to me when they're visible. I want to see black and blue, Louis, I want to see blood. Because I can't believe you even *have* blood in your veins till you show it to me. So don't come near me again, unless you've got something to show. *(Exits)*

ROY *(Looking at the door through which Joe exited)*: Every goddam thing I ever wanted they have taken from me. Mocked and reviled, all my life.

BELIZE: Join the club.

ROY: I don't belong to any club you could get through the front door of. You watch yourself you take too many liberties.

What's your name?

BELIZE *(A beat, then)*: Norman Arriaga. Belize to my friends, but you can call me Norman Arriaga.

ROY: Tell me something, Norman, you ever hire a lawyer?

BELIZE: No Roy. Never did.

ROY: Hire a lawyer, sue somebody, it's good for the soul.

Lawyers are . . . the High Priests of America. We alone know the words that made America. Out of thin air. We alone know how to use The Words. The Law: the only club I ever wanted to belong to. And before they take that from me, I'm going to die.

(Roy has a series of terrible spasms, which shake him violently. Belize approaches. Roy grabs Belize by both arms. Belize tries to pull away, but Roy hangs on, shaking them both. During this seizure, Ethel appears.)

ROY: Sssshhh. Fire. Out. *(It isn't. Violent spasms continue)* God
    have mercy. This is a lousy way to go.

BELIZE: God have mercy.

ROY *(Seeing Ethel)*: Look who's back.

BELIZE *(Looking around, seeing no one)*: Who?

ROY: Mrs. Reddy Kilowatt.

    Fucking horror. How's . . . Yonkers?

BELIZE: I almost feel sorry for you.

ETHEL: A bad idea.

ROY: Yeah. Pity. Repulsive.

    (To Belize) You. Me. *(He snaps his fingers)* No.
    Connection.

    Nobody . . . with me now. But the dead.

Scene 2

*The next day. Joe in his office at the Hall of Justice in
Brooklyn. He sits at his desk dejectedly, head in hands. Prior
and Belize enter the corridor outside.*

PRIOR *(Whisper)*: That's his office.

BELIZE *(Whisper)*: This is stupid.

PRIOR *(Whisper)*: Go home if you're chicken.

BELIZE: *You're* the one who should be home.

PRIOR: I have a hobby now: haunting people. Fuck home. You
    wait here. I want to meet my replacement.

    (He goes to Joe's door, steps in)
    Oh.

JOE: Yes, can I . . .

PRIOR: You look just like the dummy. She's right.

JOE: Who's right?

PRIOR: Your wife.

(Pause.)

JOE: What?
　　Do you know my . . .
PRIOR: No.
JOE: You said my wife.
PRIOR: No I didn't.
JOE: Yes you did.
PRIOR: You misheard. I'm a Prophet.
JOE: What?
PRIOR: PROPHET PROPHET I PROPHESY I HAVE
　　SIGHT I *SEE.*
　　　What do *you* do?
JOE: I'm a clerk.
PRIOR: Oh big deal. A clerk. You *what*, you file things? Well
　　you better be keeping a file on the hearts you break, that's
　　all that counts in the end, you'll have bills to pay in the
　　world to come, you and your friend, the Whore of
　　Babylon.
　　　(Pause)
　　　Sorry wrong room.
　　　(Exits, goes to Belize)
　　　(Despairing) He's the Marlboro Man.
BELIZE: Oooh, I wanna see.

*(Belize goes to Joe's office. Joe is standing, perplexed. Belize
sees Joe and instantly recognizes him.)*

BELIZE: *SACRED* Heart of Jesus!
JOE: Now what is . . .
　　You're Roy's nurse. I recognize you, you're . . .

BELIZE: No you don't.

JOE: From the hospital. You're Roy Cohn's nurse.

BELIZE: No I'm not. Not a nurse. We all look alike to you. You all look alike to us. It's a mad mad world. Have a nice day. *(Exits, back to Prior)*

PRIOR: Home on the range?

BELIZE: Chaps and spurs. Now girl we *got* to get you home and into . . .

PRIOR: Mega-butch. He made me feel beyond nelly. Like little wispy daisies were sprouting out my ears. Little droopy wispy wilted . . .

(Joe comes out of his office.)

BELIZE: Run! Run!

JOE: Wait!

(They're cornered by Joe. Belize keeps his face averted and partly hidden by his scarf.)

JOE: What game are you playing, this is a federal courthouse. You said . . . something about my wife. Now what. . . . How do you know my . . .

PRIOR: I'm. . . . Nothing. I'm a mental patient. He's my nurse.

BELIZE: Not his nurse, I'm not a n . . .

PRIOR: We're here because my will is being contested. Um, what is that called, when they challenge your will?

JOE: Competency? But this is an appellate court.

PRIOR: And I am appealing to anyone, anyone in the universe, who will listen to me for some . . . Charity. . . . Some people are so greedy, such pigs, they have everything, health, everything, and still they want more.

JOE: You said my wife. And I want to know, is she . . .

PRIOR: TALK TO HER YOURSELF, BULLWINKLE! WHAT DO I LOOK LIKE A MARRIAGE COUNSELOR?

Oh nursey dear, fetch the medication, I'm starting to rave.

BELIZE: Pardons, Monsieur l' Avocat, nous sommes absolument Desolée.

(Prior blows a raspberry at Joe.)

BELIZE: Behave yourself, cherie, or nanny will have to use the wooden spoon.

(Prior exits.)

BELIZE *(To Joe, dropping scarf disguise)*: I am trapped in a world of white people. That's *my* problem. *(Exits)*

Scene 3

The next day. A stormy, cold late-February day. At the Bethesda Fountain in Central Park. It's drizzling. Louis is sitting on a bench in the tunnel that looks out on the fountain. Belize enters with an umbrella; as he approaches the bench he shakes the umbrella, showering Louis, then closes it and sits.

BELIZE: Nice angel.
LOUIS: What angel?
BELIZE: The fountain.
LOUIS *(Looking)*: Bethesda.
BELIZE: What's she commemorate? Louis, I'll bet you know.

LOUIS: Naval dead of the Civil War.

BELIZE: The Civil War. I knew you'd know. You are nothing if not well informed.

LOUIS: This is Prior's favorite place in the park.

Listen I saw him yesterday. Prior.

BELIZE: Prior is *upset*.

LOUIS: Is he OK? He seemed . . . well not himself, he seemed . . .

BELIZE: Crazy?

LOUIS: Is he having . . . is he delusional, or . . .

BELIZE: With a little help from his friends.

LOUIS: Listen, this guy I'm seeing, I'm not seeing him now. Prior misunderstood, he jumped to . . .

BELIZE: Oh yeah. Your new beau. Prior and me, we went to the courthouse. Scoped him out.

LOUIS: *You had no right to do that.*

BELIZE: Oh did we violate your *rights*. What did you drag me out here for, Louis, I don't have *time* for you. You walk out on your lover. Days don't pass before you are out on the town with somebody new. But *this* . . .

LOUIS: I'm *not* out on the. . . . I want you to tell Prior that I . . .

BELIZE: *This* is a record low: sharing your dank and dirty bed with Roy Cohn's buttboy.

(Pause.)

LOUIS: Come again?

BELIZE: Doesn't that bother you at all?

LOUIS: *Roy Cohn?* What the fuck are you. . . . I am not sharing my bed with Roy Cohn's . . .

BELIZE: Your little friend didn't tell you, huh? You and Hoss

Cartwright, it's not a verbal kind of thing, you just kick off your boots and hit the hay.

LOUIS: Joe Pitt is not Roy Cohn's. . . . Joe is a very moral man, he's not even *that* conservative, or . . . well not that *kind* of a. . . . And I don't want to continue this.

BELIZE *(Starting to go)*: Bye-bye.

LOUIS: It's not my fault that Prior left you for me.

BELIZE: I beg your pardon.

LOUIS: You have always hated me. Because you are in love with Prior and you were when I met him and he fell in love with me, and so now you cook up this. . . . I mean how do you know this? That Joe and *Roy Cohn* are . . .

BELIZE: I don't know whether Mr. Cohn has penetrated more than his spiritual sphincter. All I'm saying is you better hope there's no GOP germ, Louis, 'cause if there is, you got it.

LOUIS: *I don't believe you.* Not *Roy Cohn.* He's like the polestar of human evil, he's like the worst human being who ever lived, he isn't *human* even, he's. . . . You think everything is black and white, good and evil, just because somebody is a Republican they're in bed with Roy Cohn. People like you finally fail to have an adequately grown-up, nuanced view of the world, you're Manichean, Joe is . . . well, sort of past ideology, not just another lost ineffectual leftie like me, moaning all the time about history and guilt, because this is a new era, you know, things are different now, uglier, scarier, I mean the rest of us should just surrender, just surrender, just give the fuck up, I mean. . . . *Oh god. I am so fucking wet and miserable.*

BELIZE: Finished?

LOUIS: And he. . . . And . . .

BELIZE: And he's a clerk for a Republican federal judge.

You know what your problem is, Louis? Your problem is that you are so full of piping hot crap that the mention of your name draws flies.

Just so's the record's straight: I love Prior but I was never in love with him. I have a man, uptown, and I have since *long* before I first laid my eyes on the sorry-ass sight of you.

LOUIS: I . . . I didn't know that you . . .

BELIZE: No 'cause you never bothered to ask.

Up in the air, just like that angel, too far off the earth to pick out the details. Louis and his Big Ideas. Big Ideas are all you love. "America" is what Louis loves.

(Little pause.)

LOUIS: So what? Maybe I do. You don't know what I love. You don't.

BELIZE: Well I hate America, Louis. I hate this country. It's just big ideas, and stories, and people dying, and people like you.

The white cracker who wrote the national anthem knew what he was doing. He set the word "free" to a note so high nobody can reach it. That was deliberate. Nothing on earth sounds less like freedom to me.

You come with me to room 1013 over at the hospital, I'll show you America. Terminal, crazy and mean.

(A rumble of thunder.)

BELIZE: I *live* in America, Louis, that's hard enough, I don't have to love it. You do that. Everybody's got to love something.

LOUIS: Everybody does.

Scene 4

Same day. Hannah at the Visitor's Center. Joe enters. They look at each other for a long moment.

JOE: How is she?

HANNAH: Nothing surprising.

JOE: Is she OK?

HANNAH: Well *that* would be surprising. Wouldn't it? Can I . . .

JOE: There is no possible thing I can imagine you doing. Ma. You shouldn't have come.

HANNAH: You already made that clear as day. For a month now. You can't even return a simple phone call.

JOE: A phone call from you . . . is not so simple.

HANNAH: Just so I would have something to tell her. You've been living on some rainy rooftop for all we knew. It's cruel.

JOE: Not intended to be.

HANNAH: You're sure about that.

JOE *(A beat, then)*: I'm taking her home.

HANNAH: You think that's best for her, you think that she . . .

JOE: I . . . know what I'm doing.

HANNAH: I don't think you have a clue. Which is only typical of you. You're a man, you botch up, it's not such a big deal, but she . . .

JOE: Just being a man doesn't . . .

HANNAH: Being a woman's harder. Look at her.

JOE *(A beat, then, softly)*: It's a big deal, Ma, botching up. I could use some . . .

HANNAH: Sympathy?

(Little pause)

If I could manage any, you'd just push it away. You want sympathy? Then why'd you come here?

JOE: I migrated across the breadth of the continent of North America, I ran all this way to get away from . . . *(He stops)* Is she . . . ?

HANNAH: She's not here.

JOE: But . . . she's not at the apartment, I . . .

HANNAH *(A beat, then)*: Then she escaped. Good for her.

Ask yourself what it was you were running from. It's time you did. Not from me, I was nothing. From what? And what are you running from now?

JOE: You and me. It's like we're back in Salt Lake again. You sort of bring the desert with you.

(Little pause)

Are you. . . . Don't cry.

HANNAH: If I ever do. I promise you you'll not be privileged to witness it.

JOE: It was a mistake. I should never have called you. Ma. You should never have come. I can't imagine why you did.

(Joe exits. Hannah sits. Prior enters.)

PRIOR: That man who was just here.

HANNAH *(Not looking at him)*: We're closed. Go away.

PRIOR: He's your son.

(Hannah looks at Prior. Little pause. Prior turns to leave.)

HANNAH: Do you know him. That man?

(Little pause)

How do you know that . . .

PRIOR: My ex-boyfriend, he knows him, *now*—I wanted to warn your son about *later*, when his hair goes and there's hips and jowls and all that . . . human stuff, that poor slob there's just gonna wind up miserable, fat, frightened and *alone* because Louis, he can't handle bodies.

HANNAH *(A beat, then)*: Are you a . . . a homosexual?

PRIOR: Oh is it *that* obvious? Yes. I am. What's it to you?

HANNAH: Would you say you are a typical homosexual?

PRIOR: Me? Oh I'm *stereotypical.* What, you mean like am I a hairdresser or . . .

HANNAH: Are you a hairdresser?

PRIOR: Well it would be *your* lucky day if I was because frankly . . .

    I'm sick. I'm sick. It's expensive.

    (He starts to cry)

    Oh shit now I won't be able to stop, now it's started. I feel really terrible, do I have a fever? *(Offering his forehead, impatiently)*

    Do I have a fever?

(She hesitates, then puts her hand on his forehead.)

HANNAH: Yes.

PRIOR: How high?

HANNAH: There might be a thermometer in the . . .

PRIOR: Very high, very high, could you get me to a cab, I think I want . . . *(He sits heavily on the floor)* Don't be alarmed, it's worse than it looks, I mean . . .

HANNAH: You should. . . . Try to stand up, or . . . let me see if anyone can . . .

PRIOR *(Listening to his lungs)*: Sssshhh.

    Echo-breath, it's . . . *(He shakes his head "no good")* I . . . overdid it. I'm in trouble again.

Take me to St. Vincent's Hospital, I mean, help me to a cab to the . . .

(Little pause, then Hannah exits and reenters with her coat on.)

HANNAH: Can you stand up?
PRIOR: You don't. . . . Call me a . . .
HANNAH: I'm useless here.

(She helps him stand.)

PRIOR: Please, if you're trying to convert me this isn't a good time.

(Distant thunder.)

HANNAH: Lord, look at it out there. It's pitch-black. Storm's coming in. We better move.

(They exit. Thunder.)

Scene 5

Same day, late afternoon. Harper is standing in an icy wind at the railing of the Promenade in Brooklyn Heights, staring at the river and the Manhattan skyline. The rain is falling. She is wearing a dress, inadequate for the weather, and she's barefoot. Joe enters with an umbrella. They stare at each other. Then Harper turns to face the skyline.

HARPER: The end of the world is at hand. Hello, paleface. Nothing like storm clouds over Manhattan to get you in the mood for Judgment Day.

(Thunder.)

JOE: It's freezing, it's starting to rain, where are your shoes?

HARPER: I threw them in the river.

The Judgment Day. Everyone will think they're crazy now, not just me, everyone will see things. Sick men will see angels, women who *have* houses will sell their houses, dimestore dummies will rear up on their wood-putty legs and roam the land, looking for brides.

JOE: Let's go home.

HARPER: Where's that?

(Pointing towards Manhattan) Want to buy an island? It's going out of business. You can have it for the usual cheap trinkets. Fire sale. The prices are insane.

JOE: Harper.

HARPER: Joe.

(A beat.)

Did you miss me?

JOE: I. . . . I've come back.

HARPER: Oh I know.

Here's why I wanted to stay in Brooklyn. The Promenade view.

Water won't ever accomplish the end. No matter how much you cry. Flood's not the answer, people just float. Let's go home.

Fire's the answer. The Great and Terrible Day. At last.

Scene 6

Night. Prior, Emily and Hannah in an examination room in St. Vincent's emergency room. Emily is listening to Prior's breathing while Hannah sits in a nearby chair.

EMILY: You've lost eight pounds. Eight pounds! I know people who would kill to be in the shape you were in, you were *recovering*, and you threw it away.

PRIOR: This isn't about WEIGHT, it's about LUNGS, UM . . . PNEUMONIA.

EMILY: We don't know yet.

PRIOR: THE FUCK WE DON'T ASSHOLE YOU MAY NOT BUT I *CAN'T BREATHE*.

HANNAH: You'd breathe better if you didn't holler like that.

PRIOR *(Looks at Hannah, then)*: This is my ex-lover's lover's Mormon mother.

(Little pause.)

EMILY: Even in New York in the eighties, *that* is strange.
Keep breathing. Stop moving. STAY PUT. *(She exits)*

HANNAH *(Standing to go)*: I should go.

PRIOR: I'm not insane.

HANNAH: I didn't say you . . .

PRIOR: I saw an angel. That's insane.

HANNAH: Well, it's . . .

PRIOR: Insane. But I'm not insane. But then why did I do this to myself? Because I have been driven insane by . . . your son and by that lying. . . . Because ever since She arrived, ever since, I have been consumed by this ice-cold, razorblade terror that just shouts and shouts "Keep moving! Run!" And I've run myself. . . . Into the ground. Right where She said I'd eventually be.

　　She seemed so real. What's happened to me?

(Little pause.)

HANNAH: You had a vision.

PRIOR: A vision. Thank you, Maria Ouspenskaya.

　　I'm not so far gone I can be assuaged by pity and lies.

HANNAH: I don't have pity. It's just not something I have.

　　(Little pause)

　　One hundred and seventy years ago, which is recent, an angel of God appeared to Joseph Smith in upstate New York, not far from here. People have visions.

PRIOR: But that's preposterous, that's . . .

HANNAH: It's not polite to call other people's beliefs preposterous.

　　He had great need of understanding. Our Prophet. His desire made prayer. His prayer made an angel. The angel was real. I believe that.

PRIOR: I don't. And I'm sorry but it's repellent to me. So much of what you believe.

HANNAH: What do I believe?

PRIOR: I'm a homosexual. With AIDS. I can just imagine what you . . .

HANNAH: No you can't. Imagine. The things in my head. You don't make assumptions about me, mister; I won't make them about you.

PRIOR *(A beat; he looks at her, then)*: Fair enough.

HANNAH: My son is . . . well, like you.

PRIOR: Homosexual.

HANNAH (*A nod, then*): I flew into a rage when he told me, mad as hornets. At first I assumed it was about his . . . (*She shrugs*)

PRIOR: Homosexuality.

HANNAH: But that wasn't it. Homosexuality. It just seems . . . ungainly. Two men together. It isn't an appetizing notion but then, for me, men in *any* configuration . . . well they're so lumpish and stupid. And stupidity gets me cross.

PRIOR: I wish you would be more true to your demographic profile. Life is confusing enough.

(*Little pause. They look at each other.*)

PRIOR: You know the Bible, you know . . .

HANNAH: Reasonably well, I . . .

PRIOR: The prophets in the Bible, do they . . . ever refuse their vision?

HANNAH: There's scriptural precedent, yes.

PRIOR: And what does God do to them? When they do that?

HANNAH: He. . . . Well, he feeds them to whales.

(*They both laugh. Prior's laugh brings on breathing trouble.*)

HANNAH: Just lie still. You'll be all right.

PRIOR: No. I won't be. My lungs are getting tighter. The fever mounts and you get delirious. And then days of delirium and awful pain and drugs; you start slipping and then.
I really . . . fucked up. I'm scared. I can't do it again.

HANNAH: You shouldn't talk that way. You ought to make a better show of yourself.

PRIOR: Look at this . . . horror. *(He shows her a lesion, the same one on his arm he showed Louis in Act One of* Millennium. *Then he pulls up his shirt, revealing more)*

See? That's not human. That's why I run. Wouldn't you? Wouldn't anybody.

HANNAH: It's a cancer. Nothing more. Nothing more human than that.

PRIOR: Oh God, I want to be done.

(To heaven) I want to be done.

HANNAH: An angel is just a belief, with wings and arms that can carry you. It's naught to be afraid of. If it lets you down, reject it. Seek for something new.

PRIOR: I . . .

(He stirs uncomfortably, adjusts his lap)

Oh my.

HANNAH: What?

PRIOR: Listen.

(Distant thunder.)

PRIOR: It's Her. Oh my God.

HANNAH: It's the spring rain is all.

PRIOR: No. She's coming for me now. She said she would.

Stay with me.

HANNAH: Oh no, I . . .

PRIOR: You comfort me, you do, you stiffen my spine.

HANNAH: When I got up this morning this is not how I envisioned the day would end.

I'm not needed elsewhere.

PRIOR: If I sleep, will you keep watch?

She's approaching.

HANNAH: She is?

PRIOR *(Nodding his head yes)*: Modesty forbids my explaining exactly *how* I know, but I have an infallible barometer of her proximity.

And it's rising.

Scene 7

That night. Harper and Joe at home, in bed. A silence, then:

HARPER: When we have sex. Why do you keep your eyes closed?

JOE: I don't.

HARPER: You always do. You can say why, I already know the answer.

JOE: Then why do I have to . . .

HARPER: You imagine things.

Imagine men.

JOE: Yes.

HARPER: Imagining, just like me, except the only time I wasn't imagining was when I was with you. You, the one part of the real world I wasn't allergic to.

JOE: Please. Don't.

HARPER: But I only *thought* I wasn't dreaming.

(Joe sits up abruptly, turns his back to her. Then he starts to put on his pants.)

HARPER: Oh. Oh. Back in Brooklyn, back with . . .

JOE *(Not looking at her)*: I'm going out. I have to get some stuff I left behind.

HARPER: Look at me.

(He doesn't. He keeps dressing.)

HARPER: Look at me.
　　　Look at me.
　　　(Loud) HERE! LOOK HERE AT . . .
JOE *(Looking at her)*: *What?*
HARPER: What do you see?
JOE: What do I . . . ?
HARPER: What do you see?
JOE: *Nothing,* I . . .

　　　(Little pause.)

HARPER: Thank you.
JOE: For what?
HARPER: The truth.
JOE *(A beat, then)*: I'm going. Out. Just. . . . Out. *(He exits)*
HARPER: Goodbye.

Scene 8

*Later that night. Louis in his apartment. He has a thick file
full of Xeroxed articles. He is reading. Joe enters. They stare
at each other.*

LOUIS: Have you no decency, sir? At long last? Have you no
　　　sense of decency?
　　　Who said that?
JOE: Who said . . . ?
LOUIS: Who said, "Have you no . . ."
JOE: I don't. . . . I've come back.
　　　Please let me in.

LOUIS: You're in.

JOE: I'm having a very hard time, Louis.

It's so good to see you again.

LOUIS: You *really* don't know who said, "Have you no decency?"

JOE: What's wrong? Why are you . . .

LOUIS: OK, second question: *Have* you no decency?

Guess what I spent the rainy afternoon doing?

JOE: What?

LOUIS: My homework. Research at the courthouse. Look what I got: the Decisions of Judge Theodore Wilson, Second Circuit Court of Appeals. 1981–1984. The Reagan Years.

JOE: You, um, you read my decisions.

LOUIS: *Your* decisions. Yes.

The librarian was gay, he had all the good dish, he told me that Judge Wilson didn't write these opinions any more than Nixon wrote *Six Crises* . . .

JOE: Or Kennedy wrote *Profiles in Courage.*

LOUIS: Or Reagan wrote *Where's the Rest of Me?* Or you and I wrote the Book of Love.

JOE *(Trying to soothe things, going to Louis)*: Listen, I don't want to do this now. I mean it, I need you to stop attacking and . . .

(Louis shoves Joe away, hard.)

JOE: Hey!

LOUIS: These gems were ghostwritten. By you: his obedient clerk. Naturally I was eager to read them.

JOE: Free country.

LOUIS: Uh-huh. I love the one where you found against those women on Staten Island who were suing the New Jersey factory, the toothpaste-makers whose orange-colored smoke was *blinding children* . . .

JOE: Not blind, just minor irritation.

LOUIS: Three of them had to be *hospitalized. Joe.* It's sort of brilliant, in a satanic sort of way, how you conclude that these women have no right to sue under the Air and Water Protection Act because the Air and Water Protection Act doesn't protect *people*, but actually only *air and water*! Amazing!

(Flipping through the cases) Have you no decency, have you no . . .

JOE: I don't believe this. My opinions are being criticized by the guy who changes the coffee filters in the secretaries' lounge!

LOUIS: But my *absolute favorite* is this:

Stephens versus the United States: the army guy who got a dishonorable discharge—for being gay. Now as I understand it, this Stephens had told the army he was gay when he enlisted, but when he got ready to retire they booted him out. Cheat the queer of his pension.

JOE: Right. And he sued. And he won the case. He got the pension back. So what are you . . .

LOUIS: The first judges gave him his pension back, *yes*, because: they ruled that gay men are members of a legitimate minority, entitled to the special protection of the Fourteenth Amendment of the U.S. Constitution. Equal Protection under the Law.

I can just imagine how the news of that momentary lapse into decency was received. So then all the judges on the Second Circuit were assembled, and . . .

JOE: We found for the guy again.

LOUIS: But but but!

On an equitable estoppel. I had to look that up, I'm Mr. Coffee, I can't be expected to know these things.

They didn't change the *decision*, they just changed the *reason for* the decision. Right? They gave it to him on a technicality: The army knew Stephens was gay when he enlisted. That's all, that's why he won. Not because it's unconstitutional to discriminate against homosexuals. Because homosexuals, they write, are *not* entitled to equal protection under the law.

JOE: You're being really melodramatic, as usual, you . . .

LOUIS: Actually *they* didn't write this. You did. They gave this opinion to Wilson to write, which since they *know* he's a vegetable incapable of writing do-re-mi, was quite the vote of confidence in his industrious little clerk. This is an important bit of legal fag-bashing, isn't it? They trusted you to do it. And you didn't disappoint.

JOE: It's law not justice, it's power, not the merits of its exercise, it's not an expression of the ideal, it's . . .

LOUIS: So who said, "Have you no decency?"

JOE: I'm leaving.

LOUIS: You moron, how can you not know that?

JOE *(Overlapping)*: I'm leaving, you . . . son of a bitch, get out of my . . .

LOUIS: It's only the greatest punchline in American history.

JOE: Out of my way, Louis.

LOUIS: *"Have you no decency, at long last, sir, have you no decency at all?"*

JOE: I DON'T KNOW WHO SAID IT! WHY ARE YOU DOING THIS TO ME! *I LOVE YOU. I LOVE YOU.* WHY . . .

LOUIS: JOSEPH WELCH, THE ARMY/McCARTHY HEARINGS. Ask ROY. He'll tell you. He knows. He was *there*.

Roy Cohn. What I want to know is, did you fuck him?

JOE: Did I what?

LOUIS: How often has the latex-sheathed cock I put in my mouth been previously in the mouth of the most evil, twisted, vicious bastard ever to snort coke at Studio 54, because lips that kissed those lips will never kiss mine.

JOE: Don't worry about that, just get out of the . . .

(Joe tries to push Louis aside; Louis pushes back, forcefully.)

LOUIS: Did you fuck him, did he pay you to let him . . .

JOE: MOVE!

(Louis throws the Xeroxes in Joe's face. They fly everywhere. Joe pushes Louis, Louis grabs Joe.)

LOUIS: You *lied* to me, you *love* me, well fuck you, you cheap piece of . . .

(Joe slugs Louis in the stomach, hard. Louis goes to his knees, then starts to stand up again, badly winded.)

LOUIS: He's got AIDS! Did you even *know* that? Stupid closeted bigots, you probably never figured out that each other was . . .

JOE: Shut up. *(He punches Louis again)*

LOUIS: Fascist hypocrite lying filthy . . .

(Louis tries to hit Joe, and Joe starts to hit Louis repeatedly. Louis clings to Joe as he punches away.)

LOUIS: Oh jesus, aw jeez, oh . . .

(Louis falls to the floor. Joe stands over him.)

JOE: Now stop. . . . Now stop. . . . I . . .
> Please. Say you're OK, please. *Please.*

LOUIS *(Not moving)*: That. . . . Hurt.

JOE: I never did that before, I never hit anyone before, I . . .

(Louis sits up. His mouth and eye have been cut.)

JOE: Can you open it? Can you see?

LOUIS: I can see blood.

JOE: Let me get a towel, let me . . .

LOUIS *(Pushing Joe away)*: I could have you arrested you. . . .
> Creep.
> They'd think I put you in jail for beating me up.

JOE: I never hit anyone before, I . . .

LOUIS: But it'd really be for those decisions.
> It was like a sex scene in an Ayn Rand novel, huh?

JOE: I hurt you. I'm sorry, Louis, I never hit anyone before,
> I . . .

LOUIS: Yeah yeah get lost. Before I really lose my temper and
> hurt you back.
> I just want to lie here and bleed for a while. Do me
> good.

Scene 9

Later that night. Roy in a very serious hospital bed, monitoring machines and IV drips galore. Ethel appears.

ROY *(Singing softly)*:
> John Brown's body lies a-moulderin' in the grave,
> John Brown's body lies a-moulderin' in the grave,

John Brown's body lies a-moulderin' in the grave,

His truth is marching on . . .

ETHEL: Look at that big smile. What you got to smile about, Roy?

ROY: I'm going, Ethel. Finally, finally done with this world, at long long last. All mine enemies will be standing on the other shore, mouths gaping open like stupid fish, while the Almighty parts the Sea of Death and lets his Royboy cross over to Jordan. On dry land and still a lawyer.

ETHEL: Don't count your chickens, Roy.

It's over.

ROY: Over?

ETHEL: I wanted the news should come from me.

The panel ruled against you Roy.

ROY: No, no, they only started meeting two days ago.

ETHEL: They recommended disbarment.

ROY: The Executive still has to rule . . . on the recommendation, it'll take another week to sort it out and before then . . .

ETHEL: The Executive was waiting, and they ruled, one two three. They accepted the panel's recommendation.

ROY: I'm . . .

ETHEL: One of the main guys on the Executive leaned over to his friend and said, "Finally. I've hated that little faggot for thirty-six years."

ROY: I'm. . . . They . . .

ETHEL: They won, Roy. You're not a lawyer anymore.

ROY: But am I dead?

ETHEL: No. They beat you. You lost.

(Pause)

I decided to come here so I could see could I forgive you. You who I have hated so terribly I have borne my hatred for you up into the heavens and made a needlesharp little star in the sky out of it. It's the star of Ethel Rosenberg's Hatred, and it burns every year for one night only, June Nineteen. It burns acid green.

I came to forgive but all I can do is take pleasure in your misery. Hoping I'd get to see you die more terrible than I did. And you are, 'cause you're dying in shit, Roy, defeated. And you could kill me, but you couldn't ever defeat me. You never won. And when you die all anyone will say is: better he had never lived at all.

(Pause.)

ROY: Ma?

Muddy? Is it . . . ?
(He sits up, looks at Ethel) Ma?
ETHEL *(Uncertain, then)*: It's Ethel, Roy.
ROY: Muddy? I feel bad.
ETHEL *(Looking around)*: Who are you talking to, Roy, it's . . .
ROY: Good to see you, Ma, it's been years.

I feel bad. Sing to me.
ETHEL: I'm not your mother Roy.
ROY: It's cold in here, I'm up so late, past my time.

Don't be mad Ma but I'm scared . . . ? A little.
Don't be mad. Sing me a song. Please.
ETHEL: I don't want to Roy, I'm not your . . .
ROY: Please, it's scary out here. *(He starts to cry)*
(He sinks back) Oh God. Oh God, I'm so sorry . . .

(Pause.)

ETHEL *(Singing, very soft)*:
Shteit a bocher
Un er tracht,

Tracht un tracht
A gantze nacht:
Vemen tzu nemen
Um nit farshemen
Vemen tsu nemen,
Um nit farshem.
Tum-ba-la, Tum-ba-la, Tum-balalaike,
Tum-ba-la, Tum-ba-la, Tum-balalaike,
Tum balalaike, shpil balalaike . . .
(Pause)
Roy . . . ? Are you . . . ?
(She crosses to the bed, looks at him. Goes back to her chair)
That's it.

(Belize enters, goes to the bed.)

BELIZE: Wake up, it's time to . . .
Oh. Oh, you're . . .
ROY *(Sitting up violently)*: No I'm NOT!
I fooled you Ethel, I knew who you were all along, I can't believe you fell for that ma stuff, I just wanted to see if I could finally, finally make Ethel Rosenberg sing! I WIN!
(He falls back on the bed)
Oh fuck, oh fuck me I . . .
(In a very faint voice) Next time around: I don't want to be a man. I wanna be an octopus. Remember that, OK? A fucking . . . *(Punching an imaginary button with his finger)* Hold.
(He dies)

ACT FIVE:

Heaven, I'm in Heaven

February 1986

Scene 1

Very late, same night. Prior's hospital room. Hannah is sleeping in a chair. Prior is standing on his bed. There's an eerie light on him. Hannah stirs, moans a little, wakes up suddenly, sees him.

PRIOR: She's on her way.

(The lights drain to black.)

HANNAH: Turn the lights back on, turn the lights . . .

(There is the sound of a silvery trumpet in the dark, and a tattoo of faraway drums. Silence. Thunder. Then all over the walls, Hebrew letters appear, writhing in flames. The Angel is there, suddenly. She is dressed in black and looks terrifying. Hannah screams and buries her face in her hands.)

ANGEL:

I I I I Have Returned, Prophet,

(Thunder.)

ANGEL:

And not according to Plan.

PRIOR: Take it back.

(Big thunderclap.)

PRIOR: The Book, whatever you left in me, I won't be its repository, I reject it.

(Thunder.)

PRIOR *(To Hannah)*: Help me out here. HELP ME!

HANNAH *(Trying to shut it all out)*: I don't, I don't, this is a dream it's a dream it's a . . .

PRIOR: I don't think that's really the point right at this particular moment.

HANNAH: I don't know what to . . .

PRIOR *(Overlap)*: Well it was your idea, reject the vision you said and . . .

HANNAH *(Overlap)*: Yes but I thought it was more a . . . metaphorical. . . . I . . .

PRIOR *(Overlap)*: You said scriptural precedent, you said. . . . WHAT AM I SUPPOSED TO . . .

HANNAH *(Overlap)*: You . . . you . . . wrestle her.

PRIOR: SAY *WHAT*?

HANNAH: It's an angel, you . . . just . . . grab hold and say . . . oh what was it, wait, wait, umm. . . . OH! Grab her, say "I will not let thee go except thou bless me!" Then wrestle with her till she gives in.

PRIOR: YOU wrestle her, I don't know how to wrestle, I . . .

(The Angel flies up into the air and lands right in front of Prior. Prior grabs her—she emits a terrible, impossibly loud, shuddering eagle-screech. Prior and the Angel wrestle. The wrestling should begin in earnest and rapidly become furious, deadly. As Prior gains the upper hand, he begins to speak.)

PRIOR: I . . . will not let thee go except thou bless me. Take back your Book. Anti-Migration, that's so feeble, I can't believe you couldn't do better than that, free me, unfetter me, bless me or whatever but I will be let go.

ANGEL *(Taking to the air, trying to escape; a whole chorus of voices)*:

> I I I I Am the
> CONTINENTAL PRINCIPALITY OF AMER-
> ICA, I I I I
> AM THE BIRD OF PREY I Will NOT BE COM-
> PELLED, I . . .

(There is a great blast of music and a shaft of white light streams in through the blue murk. Within this incredibly bright column of light there is a ladder of even brighter, purer light, reaching up into infinity. At the conjunctions of each rung there are flaming alephs.)

ANGEL:

> Entrance has been gained. Return the Text to Heaven.

PRIOR *(Terrified)*: Can I come back? I don't want to go unless . . .

ANGEL *(Angry)*:

> You have prevailed, Prophet. You. . . . Choose.

Now release me.

I have torn a muscle in my thigh.

PRIOR: Big deal, my leg's been hurting for months.

(He releases the Angel. He hesitates. He ascends. The room is instantly plunged into near darkness. The Angel turns her attention to Hannah.)

HANNAH: What? What? You've got no business with me, I didn't call you, you're *his* fever dream not mine, and he's gone now and you should go too, I'm waking up right . . . NOW!

(Nothing happens. The Angel spreads her wings. The room becomes red hot. The Angel extends her hands towards Hannah. Hannah walks towards her, and kneels. The Angel kisses her on the forehead and then the lips—a long, hot kiss.)

ANGEL: The Body is the Garden of the Soul.

(Hannah has an enormous orgasm as the Angel flies away to the accompanying glissando of a baroque piccolo trumpet.)

Scene 2

Prior Walter is in Heaven. He is dressed in prophet robes reminiscent of Charlton Heston's Moses drag in The Ten Commandments. *He is carrying the Book of the Anti-Migratory Epistle. Heaven looks mostly like San Francisco after the Great 1906 Quake. It has a deserted, derelict feel to it, rubble is strewn everywhere. Seated on a wooden crate on a street corner is Harper, playing with a cat.*

HARPER: Oh! It's you! My imaginary friend.

PRIOR: What are you doing here? Are you dead?

HARPER: No, I just had sex, I'm not dead! Why? Where are we?

PRIOR: Heaven.

HARPER: Heaven? I'm in Heaven?

PRIOR: That cat! That's Little Sheba!

HARPER: She was wandering around. Everyone here wanders. Or they sit on crates, playing card games. Heaven. Holy moly.

PRIOR: How did Sheba die?

HARPER: Rat poison, hit by a truck, fight with an alley cat, cancer, another truck, old age, fell in the East River, heartworms and one last truck.

PRIOR: Then it's true? Cats really have nine lives?

HARPER: That was a joke. I don't know how she died, I don't talk to cats I'm not that crazy. Just upset. We had sex, and then he . . . had to go. I drank an enormous glass of water and two Valiums. Or six. Maybe I overdosed, like Marilyn Monroe.

PRIOR: She didn't OD, she was assassinated by Jimmy Hoffa and JFK.

HARPER: Threshold of revelation?

PRIOR *(Shaking his head no)*: The Phil Donahue show.

HARPER: Did you die?

PRIOR: No, I'm here on business.

HARPER: What kind of business?

PRIOR: I have to choose. I can return to the world. If I want to.

HARPER: Do you?

PRIOR: I don't know.

HARPER: I know. Heaven is depressing, full of dead people and all, but life.

It's all a matter of the opposable thumb and forefinger; not of the hand but of the heart; we grab hold like nobody's business and then we don't seem to be able to let go.

PRIOR: To face loss. With grace. Is key, I think, but it's impossible. All you ever do is lose, and lose . . .

HARPER: But not letting go deforms you so.

PRIOR: The world's too hard. Stay here. With me.

HARPER: I can't. I feel like shit but I've never felt more alive. I've finally found the secret of all that Mormon energy. Devastation. That's what makes people migrate, build things. Heartbroken people do it, people who have lost love. Because I don't think God loves His people any better than Joe loved me. The string was cut, and off they went.

I have to go now. I'm ready to lose him. Armed with the truth. He's got a sweet hollow center, but he's the nothing man.

I hope you come back. *Look* at this place. Can you imagine spending eternity here?

PRIOR: It's supposed to look like San Francisco.

HARPER *(Looking around:)*: Ugh.

PRIOR: Oh but the real San Francisco, on earth, is unspeakably beautiful.

HARPER: Unspeakable beauty.

That's something I would like to see.

(Harper and Sheba vanish.)

PRIOR: Oh! She. . . . She took the cat. Come back, you took the . . .

(Little pause)

Goodbye Little Sheba. Goodbye.

(The scenery dissolves and is replaced by an interior. A great antechamber to the Hall of the Upper Orders. It looks remarkably like the San Francisco City Hall, with much cracked plaster. The Angel is there.)

ANGEL:

Greetings, Prophet. We have been waiting for you.

Scene 3

Two AM. Roy's hospital room. Roy's body is on the bed. Ethel is sitting in a chair. Belize enters, then calls off in a whisper.

BELIZE: Hurry.

(Louis enters wearing an overcoat and dark sunglasses.)

LOUIS: Oh my god, oh my god it's—. Oh this is too weird for words, it's Roy Cohn, it's . . . so *creepy* here, I hate hospitals, I . . .

BELIZE: *Stop whining.* We have to move fast, I'm supposed to call the duty nurse if his condition changes and . . . *(He looks at Roy)* It's changed.

Take off those glasses you look ridiculous.

(Louis takes off the glasses. He has two black eyes, one cut.)

BELIZE: What happened to *you?* *(He touches the swelling near Louis's eye)*

LOUIS: OW OW! *(He waves Belize's hand away)* Expiation. For my sins.

What am I doing here?

BELIZE: Expiation for your sins. I can't take the stuff out myself, I have to tell them he's dead and fill out all the forms, and I don't want them confiscating the medicine. I needed a packmule, so I called you.

LOUIS: Why me? You hate me.

BELIZE: I needed a Jew. You were the first to come to mind.

LOUIS: What do you mean you needed . . .

BELIZE: We're going to thank him. For the pills.

LOUIS: *Thank him?*

BELIZE: What do you call the Jewish prayer for the dead?

LOUIS: The Kaddish?

BELIZE: That's the one. Hit it.

LOUIS: Whoah, hold on.

BELIZE: Do it, do it, they'll be in here to check and he . . .

LOUIS: I'm not saying any fucking Kaddish for him. The drugs OK, sure, fine, but no fucking way am I praying for *him*. My New Deal Pinko Parents in Schenectady would never forgive me, they're already so disappointed, "He's a fag. He's an office temp. And *now look*, he's saying Kaddish for Roy Cohn."

I can't believe you'd actually pray for . . .

BELIZE: Louis, I'd even pray for you.

He was a terrible person. He died a hard death. So maybe. . . . A queen can forgive her vanquished foe. It isn't easy, it doesn't count if it's easy, it's the hardest thing. Forgiveness. Which is maybe where love and justice finally meet. Peace, at least. Isn't that what the Kaddish asks for?

LOUIS: Oh it's Hebrew who knows what it's asking?

(Little pause. Louis looks at Roy, staring at him unflinchingly for the first time.)

LOUIS: I'm thirty-two years old and I've never been in a room with a dead body before. *(He touches Roy's forehead)* It's so heavy, and small. I know probably less of the Kaddish than you do, Belize, I'm an intensely secular Jew, I didn't even Bar Mitzvah.

BELIZE: Do the best you can.

(Louis puts a Kleenex on his head.)

LOUIS: Yisgadal ve'yiskadash sh'mey rabo, sh'mey de kidshoh, uh. . . . Boray pre hagoffen. No, that's the Kiddush, not the. . . . Um, shema Yisroel adonai. . . . This is silly, Belize, I can't . . .

ETHEL *(Standing, softly)*: B'olmo deevro chiroosey ve'yamlich malchusey . . .

LOUIS: B'olmo deevro chiroosey ve'yamlich malchusey . . .

ETHEL: Bechayeychon uv'yomechechon uvchayey d'chol beys Yisroel . . .

LOUIS: Bechayeychon uv'yomechechon uvchayey d'chol beys Yisroel . . .

ETHEL: Ba'agolo uvizman koriv . . .

LOUIS: Ve'imroo omain.

ETHEL: Yehey sh'mey rabo m'vorach . . .

LOUIS AND ETHEL: L'olam ulolmey olmayoh. Yisborach ve'-yishtabach ve'yispoar ve'yisroman ve'yisnasey ve'yis'hadar ve'yisalleh ve'yishallol sh'mey dekudsho . . .

ETHEL: Berich hoo le'eylo min kol birchoso veshiroso . . .

LOUIS AND ETHEL: Tushbchoso venechemoso, daameeron b'olmo ve'imroo omain. Y'he sh'lomo rabbo min sh'mayo v'chayim olenu v'al kol Yisroel, v'imru omain . . .

ETHEL: Oseh sholom bimromov, hu ya-aseh sholom olenu v'al col Yisroel . . .

LOUIS: Oseh sholom bimromov, hu ya-aseh sholom olenu v'al col Yisroel . . .

ETHEL: V'imru omain.

LOUIS: V'imru omain.

ETHEL: You sonofabitch.

LOUIS: You sonofabitch.

(Ethel vanishes.)

BELIZE: Thank you Louis, you did fine.

LOUIS: Fine? What are you talking about, fine? That was fucking miraculous.

Scene 4

Two AM. Joe enters the empty Brooklyn apartment, carrying the suitcase from Louis's.

JOE: I'm back. Harper?
   (He switches on a light.)
   Harper?

(Roy enters from the bedroom, dressed in a fabulous floor-length black velvet robe de chambre. Joe starts with terror, turns away, then looks again. Roy's still there.)

JOE: What are you doing here?

ROY: Dead Joe doesn't matter.

JOE: No, no, you're not here, you . . .
   You lied to me. You said cancer, you said . . .

ROY: You could have read it in the papers. AIDS. I didn't want you to get the wrong impression.

You feel bad that you beat somebody.

JOE: I want you to . . .

ROY: He deserved it.

JOE: No he didn't he . . .

ROY: Everybody does. Everybody could use a good beating.

JOE: I *hurt* him. I didn't . . . mean to, I didn't want to but. . . . I made him bleed. And he won't . . . ever see me again, I won't . . .

Louis.

(He starts to cry)

Oh God, please go, Roy, you're really frightening me, please please go.

HARPER.

ROY: Show me a little of what you've learned, baby Joe. Out in the world.

(Roy kisses Joe softly on the mouth.)

ROY: Damn.

I gotta shuffle off this mortal coil. I hope they have something for me to do in the Great Hereafter, I get bored easy.

You'll find, my friend, that what you love will take you places you never dreamed you'd go.

(Roy vanishes. Harper enters. Joe and Harper stare at each other.)

HARPER: Hope you didn't worry.

JOE: Harper?

Where. . . . Were you . . .

HARPER: A trip to the moon on gossamer wings.

JOE: What?

HARPER: You ought to get your hearing checked, you say that a lot.

I was out. With a friend. In Paradise.

Scene 5

Heaven: in the Council Room of the Continental Principalities. As the scene is being set, a Voice (the same one heard in Act One Scene 1 and Act Three Scene 3) proclaims:

VOICE: In the Hall of the Continental Principalities; Heaven, a City Much Like San Francisco. Six of Seven Myriad Infinite Aggregate Angelic Entities in Attendance, May Their Glorious Names Be Praised Forever and Ever, Hallelujah. Permanent Emergency Council is now in Session.

(The Continental Principalities sit around a table covered with a heavy tapestry on which is woven an ancient map of the world. The tabletop is covered with antique and broken astronomical, astrological, mathematical and nautical objects of measurement and calculation; heaps and heaps and heaps of books and files and bundles of yellowing newspapers; inkpots, clay tablets, styli and quill pens. The great chamber is dimly lit by candles and a single great bulb overhead, the light of which pulses to the audible rhythmic surgings and waverings of an unseen generator. At the center of the table is a single bulky radio, a 1940s model in very poor repair. It is switched on and glowing, and the Angels are gathered about it, intent upon its dim, crackly signal.)

RADIO *(In a British accent)*: . . . one week following the explosion at the number four reactor, the fires are still burning and an estimated . . . *(Static)* . . . the disaster at the Chernobyl Power Plant in Belarus is already by leagues the greatest nuclear catastrophe in postwar . . . *(Static)*. . . releasing into the atmosphere fifty million curies of radioactive iodine, six million curies of caesium and strontium rising in a plume over five miles high, carried by the winds over an area stretching from the Urals to thousand of miles beyond Soviet borders, it . . . *(Static)*

ASIATICA: We are losing the signal.

(The Angels make mystic gestures. The signal returns.)

RADIO: . . . falling like toxic snow into the Dnieper River, which provides drinking water for thirty-five million Russians. Radioactive debris contaminating over three hundred thousand hectares of topsoil for a minimum of thirty years, and . . . *(Static)* . . . now hearing of thousands of workers who have absorbed fifty times the lethal dose of . . . *(Static)* . . . BBC Radio, reporting live from Chernobyl, on the eighth day of the . . . *(The signal is engulfed in white noise and fades out)*

ANTARCTICA: When?

OCEANIA: April 26th. Sixty-two days from today.

AFRICANII: How will they respond to this?

EUROPA: Die horribly. In multitudes.

OCEANIA: And then build more.

EUROPA: And die. In multitudes.

ANTARCTICA *(Quietly)*: I I I will rejoice to see it.

AUSTRALIA *(A polite but firm reprimand)*: That. Is forbidden us.

ANTARCTICA: By Whom?

(Some of the Angels cough, some make mystic signs.)

ASIATICA: This radio is a terrible radio.

AFRICANII: The reception is too weak.

EUROPA: A vacuum tube is blown.

OCEANIA: Dead.

AUSTRALIA: Can it be fixed?

EUROPA: That is Beyond Us.

AFRICANII: Actually it is a simple diode. Within are an anode and a cathode. The positive electrons travel from the cathode across voltage fields . . .

ASIATICA: Diodes are the product of the selfsame antinomic, divided human consciousness which produced the multifarious catastrophes of which We are impotent witness, dichotomous, propulsive . . .

OCEANIA *(Overlapping on "witness")*: The cathode, in fact, is negatively charged.

AFRICANII: No, positive. The anode is . . .

EUROPA: This device ought never to have been brought here. It is an Abomination, it is a Pandemonium, it is . . .

OCEANIA: And without it, Oh Most Glorious Intelligences, how would we maintain surveillance over Human Mischief? With *this*? *(He brandishes an astrolabe)*

The following speeches begin independently but are more or less simultaneous and climax in chaos.

EUROPA: I I I do not want to survey, it is beneath us, these anthill excursions, and between this crippled gadget and the mephitic plumes of that human-conceived Diabolus, that *reactor*, there is not a scintilla of difference . . .

AFRICANII *(Overlapping on "anthill")*: The positive electrons travel through a. . . . They *are* negative, You are correct, I I I . . .

ANTARCTICA *(Overlapping on "reactor")*: I I I I do not weep for them, I I I I weep for the vexation of the Blank Spaces, I weep for the Dancing Light, for the irremediable wastage of Fossil Fuels, Old Blood of the Globe spilled wantonly or burned and jettisoned into the Crystal Air, I I I I delight in their suffering, I I I I will never relent, let them reap the harvest of . . .

AUSTRALIA *(Overlapping on Africanii's "positive electrons")*: If only He would return I I I I do not know whether We have erred in transporting these dubious Things but. . . . If We refer to His Codex of Procedure, I I I I cannot recall which page it was on, but He has surely provided for the Conundrum . . .

ASIATICA *(Overlapping on Europa's "Diabolus")*: TRUE! TRUE! Cathode rays were discovered in America following Einstein's publication of the Photoelectric Effect, and so Einstein is the Thread of Presumption and accursed Invention which unites these insidious interventions in the curved Web of Time and Distance which so disturbs . . .

EUROPA: Actually, it was Hayes, a European, who discovered the cathode ray, and the patent was stolen by an American who merely altered a few minor technical aspects of an inspiration which was *MINE*, and . . .

AFRICANII: Regardless of the charge, it is the absence of resistance in a vacuum which . . .

OCEANIA *(Overlapping on Antarctica's "delight in their suffering")*: And yet you *will* weep for them, Oh Heavens! Be amazed, be appalled, be warned, for IN THAT DAY, there will be more than vexation on *earth* . . .

(There is an enormous peal of thunder and a blaze of lightning. Prior and the Angel of America are in the chamber, standing before the council table. The Principalities stare at Prior.)

ANGEL: Most August Fellow Principalities, Angels Most High: I regret my absence at this session, I was detained.

(Pause.)

AUSTRALIA: Ah, this is . . . ?
ANGEL: The Prophet. Yes.
AUSTRALIA: Ah.

(The Angels bow.)

EUROPA: We were working.
AFRICANII: Making Progress.

(Thunderclap.)

PRIOR: I . . . I want to return this.

(He holds out the Book. No one takes it from him.)

AUSTRALIA: What is the matter with it?
PRIOR *(A beat, then)*: It just. . . . It just. . . . We can't just stop. We're not rocks—progress, migration, motion is . . . modernity. It's *animate*, it's what living things do. We desire. Even if all we desire is stillness, it's still desire *for*. Even if we go faster than we should. We can't *wait*. And wait for what? God . . .

(Thunderclap.)

PRIOR: God . . .

(Thunderclap.)

PRIOR: He isn't coming back.
> And even if he did . . .
> If He ever did come back, if He ever *dared* to show His face, or his Glyph or whatever in the Garden again . . . if after all this destruction, if after all the terrible days of this terrible century He returned to see . . . how much suffering His abandonment had created, if He did come back you should *sue* the bastard. That's my only contribution to all this Theology. Sue the bastard for walking out. How dare He.

(Pause.)

ANGEL: Thus spake the Prophet.
PRIOR *(Starting to put the Book on the table)*: So thank you . . . for sharing this with me, but I don't want to keep it.
OCEANIA *(To the Angel of America)*: He wants to live.
PRIOR: Yes.
> I'm thirty years old, for God sake.

(Softer rumble of thunder.)

PRIOR: I haven't *done* anything yet, I . . .
> I want to be healthy again. And this plague, it should stop. In me and everywhere. Make it go away.
AUSTRALIA:
> Oh We have tried.
> We suffer with You but

> We do not know. We
> Do not know how.

(Prior and Australia look at each other.)

EUROPA:

> This is the Tome of Immobility, of respite, of cessation.
> Drink of its bitter water once, Prophet, and never thirst again.

(Prior puts the Book on the table. He removes his prophet robes, revealing the hospital gown underneath. He places the robe by the Book.)

PRIOR: I . . . can't.

> I still want. . . . My blessing. Even sick. I want to be alive.

ANGEL:

> You only think you do.
> Life is a habit with you.
> You have not *seen* what is to come:
> We *have*:
> What will the grim Unfolding of these Latter Days bring?
> That you or any Being should wish to endure them?
> Death more plenteous than all Heaven has tears to mourn it,
> The slow dissolving of the Great Design,
> The spiraling apart of the Work of Eternity,
> The World and its beautiful particle logic
> All collapsed. All dead, forever,
> In starless, moonlorn onyx night.

(The generator begins to fail, the lights to dim.)

ANGEL:
>   We are failing, failing,
>   The Earth and the Angels.
>   Look up, look up,
>   It is Not-to-Be Time.
>   Oh who asks of the Orders Blessing
>   With Apocalypse Descending?
>   Who demands: More Life?
>   When Death like a Protector
>   Blinds our eyes, shielding from tender nerve
>   More horror than can be borne.
>   Let any Being on whom Fortune smiles
>   Creep away to Death
>   Before that last dreadful daybreak
>   When all your ravaging returns to you
>   With the rising, scorching, unrelenting Sun:
>   When morning blisters crimson
>   And bears all life away,
>   A tidal wave of Protean Fire
>   That curls around the planet
>   And bares the Earth clean as bone.

(Pause.)

PRIOR: But still. Still.
>   Bless me anyway.
>   I want more life. I can't help myself. I do.
>   I've lived through such terrible times, and there are
>   people who live through much much worse, but. . . . You
>   see them living anyway.

135

When they're more spirit than body, more sores than skin, when they're burned and in agony, when flies lay eggs in the corners of the eyes of their children, they live. Death usually has to *take* life away. I don't know if that's just the animal. I don't know if it's not braver to die. But I recognize the habit. The addiction to being alive. We live past hope. If I can find hope anywhere, that's it, that's the best I can do. It's so much not enough, so inadequate but. . . . Bless me anyway. I want more life.

(Prior begins to exit. The Angels, unseen by him, make a mystical sign. He turns again to face them.)

PRIOR: And if He returns, take Him to court. He walked out on us. He ought to pay.

Scene 6

On the streets of Heaven. Rabbi Isidor Chemelwitz and Sarah Ironson are seated on wooden crates with another crate between them. They are playing cards. Prior enters.

PRIOR: Excuse me, I'm looking for a way out of this, do you . . . Oh! You're . . .

SARAH IRONSON *(To the Rabbi)*: Vos vil er? [What does he want?]

RABBI ISIDOR CHEMELWITZ: Di goyim, zey veysn nisht vi zikh oyftsufirn. [These Gentiles, they have no manners.]

PRIOR: Are you Sarah Ironson?

(She looks up at him.)

PRIOR: I was at your funeral! You look just like your grandson, Louis. I know him. Louis. He never wanted you to find out, but did you know he's gay?

SARAH IRONSON *(Not understanding)*: Vi? [What?]

RABBI ISIDOR CHEMELWITZ: Dein aynickl, Louis? [Your grandson, Louis?]

SARAH IRONSON: Yeah?

RABBI ISIDOR CHEMELWITZ *(Sotto voce)*: Er iz a feygele. [He is a fag.]

SARAH IRONSON: A *feygele*? Oy.

RABBI ISIDOR CHEMELWITZ: Itst gistu. [You deal.]

PRIOR: Why does everyone here play cards?

RABBI ISIDOR CHEMELWITZ: Why? *(To Sarah)* Dos goy vil visn far-Vos mir shpiln in kortn. [The goy wants to know why we play cards.]

OK.

Cards is strategy but mostly a game of chance. In Heaven, everything is known. To the Great Questions are lying about here like yesterday's newspaper all the answers. So from what comes the pleasures of Paradise? *Indeterminacy!* Because mister, with the Angels, those makhers, may their names be always worshipped and adored, it's all gloom and doom and give up already. But still is there Accident, in this pack of playing cards, still is there the Unknown, the Future. You understand me? It ain't all so much mechanical as they think.

You got another question?

PRIOR: I want to go home.

RABBI ISIDOR CHEMELWITZ: Oh simple. Here. To do this, every Kabbalist on earth would sell his right nut.

Penuel, Peniel, Ja'akov Beth-Yisroel, Killeeyou, killeemee, OOO-ooooooooo-OOOO-oooooohmayn!

(The ladder, the music and the lights. Prior starts to descend.)

SARAH IRONSON: Hey! Zogt Loubeleh az di Bobbe zogt:

RABBI ISIDOR CHEMELWITZ: She says tell this Louis Grandma says:

SARAH IRONSON: Er iz tomid geven a bissele farblonjet, shoin vi a boytshikl. Ober siz nisht keyn antshuldigunk.

RABBI ISIDOR CHEMELWITZ: From when he was a boy he was always mixed up. But it's no excuse.

SARAH IRONSON: *He should have visited!* But I forgive. Tell him: az er darf ringen mit zain Libm Nomen. Yah?!

RABBI ISIDOR CHEMELWITZ: You should struggle with the Almighty!

SARAH IRONSON: Azoi toot a Yid.

RABBI ISIDOR CHEMELWITZ: It's the Jewish way.

Scene 7

As Prior journeys to earth he sees Roy, at a great distance, in Heaven, or Hell or Purgatory—standing waist-deep in a smoldering pit, facing a volcanic, pulsating red light. Underneath, a basso-profundo roar, like a thousand Bessemer furnaces going at once, deep underground.

ROY: Paternity suit? Abandonment? Family court is my particular metier, I'm an absolute fucking demon with Family Law. Just tell me who the judge is, and what kind of jewelry does he like? If it's a jury, it's harder, juries take more talk but sometimes it's worth it, going jury, for what it saves you in bribes. Yes I will represent you, King of the Universe, yes I will sing and eviscerate, I will bully and seduce, I will win for you and make the plaintiffs, those traitors, wish they had never heard the name of . . .

(Huge thunderclap.)

ROY: Is it a done deal, are we on? Good, then I gotta start by telling you you ain't got a case here, you're guilty as hell, no question, you have nothing to plead but not to worry, darling, I will make something up.

Scene 8

It's morning, the next day. Prior descends from Heaven and slips into bed. Belize is sleeping in a chair.

PRIOR *(Waking)*: Oh.
　　　I'm exhausted.
BELIZE *(Waking)*: You've been working hard.
PRIOR: I feel terrible.
BELIZE: Welcome back to the world.
PRIOR: From where, I. . . . Oh. Oh I . . .

(Emily enters.)

EMILY: Well look at this. It's the dawn of man.
BELIZE: Venus rising from the sea.
PRIOR: I'm wet.
EMILY: Fever broke. That's a good sign, they'll be in to change you in . . .
PRIOR *(Looking around)*: Mrs. Pitt? Did she . . .

BELIZE: Elle fait sa toilette. Elle est *très* formidable, ça. Where did you find her?

PRIOR: We found each other, she . . .

I've had a remarkable dream. And you were there, and you . . .

(Hannah enters.)

PRIOR: And you.

HANNAH: I what?

PRIOR: And some of it was terrible, and some of it was wonderful, but all the same I kept saying I want to go home. And they sent me home.

HANNAH *(To Prior)*: What are you talking about?

PRIOR *(To Hannah)*: Thank you.

HANNAH: I just slept in the chair.

PRIOR *(To Belize)*: She saved my life.

HANNAH: I did no such thing, I slept in the chair. Being in hospital upsets me, it reminds me of things.

I have to go home now. I had the most *peculiar* dream.

(There's a knock on the door. It opens. Louis enters.)

LOUIS: Can I come in?

(Brief tense pause; Prior looks at Louis and then at Belize.)

EMILY: I have to start rounds.

(To Prior) You're one of the lucky ones. I could give you a rose.

You rest your weary bones.

PRIOR *(To Louis)*: What are you . . .

(He sees Louis's cuts and bruises) What happened to you?

LOUIS: Visible scars. You said . . .

PRIOR: Oh Louis, you're so goddamned literal about everything.

HANNAH: I'm going now.

PRIOR: You'll come back.

HANNAH *(A beat, then)*: If I can. I have things to take care of.

PRIOR: Please do. I have always depended on the kindness of strangers.

HANNAH: Well that's a stupid thing to do. *(Exits)*

LOUIS: Who's she?

PRIOR *(A beat, then)*: You really don't want to know.

BELIZE: Before I depart. A homecoming gift.

(Belize puts his shoulder bag in Prior's lap. Prior opens it; it's full of bottles of pills.)

PRIOR *(Squinting hard)*: What? I can't read the label, I . . .
My eyes. Aren't any better.
(Squints even harder) AZT?
Where on earth did you. . . . These are hot pills. I am shocked.

BELIZE: A contribution to the get-well fund. From a bad fairy.

LOUIS: These pills, they . . . they make you better.

PRIOR: They're poison, they make you anemic.
This is my life, from now on, Louis. I'm not getting "better."
(To Belize) I'm not sure I'm ready to do that to my bone marrow.

BELIZE *(Taking the bag)*: We can talk about it tomorrow. I'm going home to nurse my grudges. Ta, baby, sleep all day. Ta, Louis, you sure know how to clear a room. *(He exits)*

LOUIS: Prior.

I want to come back to you.

Scene 9

Same morning. Split scene: Louis and Prior in Prior's hospital room, as before; Harper and Joe in Brooklyn, as at the end of Act Five Scene 4.

HARPER: I want your credit card.

That's all. You can keep track of me from where the charges come from. If you want to keep track. I don't care.

JOE: I have some things to tell you.

HARPER: Oh we shouldn't talk. I don't want to do that anymore.

Credit card.

JOE: I don't know what will happen to me without you. Only you. Only you love me. Out of everyone in the world. I have done things, I'm ashamed. But I have changed. I don't know how yet, but. . . . Please, please, don't leave me now.

Harper.

You're my good heart.

(She looks at him, she walks up to him and slaps him, hard.)

HARPER *(Quietly)*: Did that hurt?

(Joe nods yes.)

HARPER: Yes. Remember that. Please.

If I can get a job, or something, I'll cut the card to pieces. And there won't be charges anymore. Credit card.

(Joe takes out his wallet, gives her his card.)

JOE *(Small voice, not looking at her)*: Call or. . . . Call. You have to.

HARPER: No. Probably never again. That's how bad.

Sometimes, maybe lost is best. Get lost. Joe. Go exploring.

(She digs in the sofa. She removes her Valium stash. She shakes out two pills, goes to Joe, takes his hand and puts the Valium in his open palm)

With a big glass of water. *(She leaves)*

LOUIS: I want to come back to you.

You could . . . respond, you could say something, throw me out or say it's fine, or it's not fine but sure what the hell or . . .

(Little pause)

I really failed you. But . . . this is hard. Failing in love isn't the same as not loving. It doesn't let you off the hook, it doesn't mean . . . you're free to not love.

PRIOR: I love you Louis.

LOUIS: Good. I love you.

PRIOR: I really do.

But you can't come back. Not ever.

I'm sorry. But you can't.

Scene 10

That night. Louis and Prior remain from the previous scene. Joe is sitting alone in Brooklyn. Harper appears. She is in a window seat on board a jumbo jet, airborne.

HARPER: Night flight to San Francisco. Chase the moon across America.

God! It's been years since I was on a plane!

When we hit thirty-five thousand feet, we'll have reached the tropopause. The great belt of calm air. As close as I'll ever get to the ozone.

I dreamed we were there. The plane leapt the tropopause, the safe air, and attained the outer rim, the ozone, which was ragged and torn, patches of it threadbare as old cheesecloth, and that was frightening . . .

But I saw something only I could see, because of my astonishing ability to see such things:

Souls were rising, from the earth far below, souls of the dead, of people who had perished, from famine, from war, from the plague, and they floated up, like skydivers in reverse, limbs all akimbo, wheeling and spinning. And the souls of these departed joined hands, clasped ankles, and formed a web, a great net of souls, and the souls were three-atom oxygen molecules, of the stuff of ozone, and the outer rim absorbed them, and was repaired.

Nothing's lost forever. In this world, there is a kind of painful progress. Longing for what we've left behind, and dreaming ahead.

At least I think that's so.

EPILOGUE:

Bethesda

February 1990

Prior, Louis, Belize and Hannah sitting on the rim of the Bethesda Fountain in Central Park. It's a bright day, but cold. Prior is heavily bundled, and he has thick glasses on and supports himself with a cane. Hannah is noticeably different—she looks like a New Yorker, and she is reading the New York Times. *Louis and Belize are arguing. The Bethesda Angel is above them all.*

LOUIS: The Berlin Wall has fallen. The Ceausescus are out. He's building democratic socialism. The New Internationalism. Gorbachev is the greatest political thinker since Lenin.

BELIZE: I don't think we know enough yet to start canonizing him. The Russians hate his guts.

LOUIS: Yeah but. Remember back four years ago? The whole time we were feeling everything everywhere was stuck, while in Russia! Look! Perestroika! The Thaw! It's the end of the Cold War! The whole world is changing! Overnight!

HANNAH: I wonder what'll happen now in places like Czechoslovakia and Yugoslavia.

LOUIS: Yugoslavia?

PRIOR *(To audience)*: Let's just turn the volume down on this, OK?

They'll be at it for hours. It's not that what they're saying isn't important, it's just . . .

This is my favorite place in New York City. No, in the whole universe. The parts of it I have seen.

On a day like today. A sunny winter's day, warm and cold at once. The sky's a little hazy, so the sunlight has a physical presence, a character. In autumn, those trees across the lake are yellow, and the sun strikes those most brilliantly. Against the blue of the sky, that sad fall blue, those trees are more light than vegetation. They are Yankee trees, New England transplants. They're barren now. It's January 1990. I've been living with AIDS for five years. That's six whole months longer than I lived with Louis.

LOUIS: Whatever comes, what you have to admire in Gorbachev, in the Russians is that they're making a leap into the unknown. You can't wait around for a theory. The sprawl of life, the weird . . .

HANNAH: Interconnectedness . . .

LOUIS: Yes.

BELIZE: Maybe the sheer size of the terrain.

LOUIS: It's all too much to be encompassed by a single theory now.

BELIZE: The world is faster than the mind.

LOUIS: That's what politics is. The world moving ahead. And only in politics does the miraculous occur.

BELIZE: But that's a theory.

HANNAH: You need an idea of the world to go out into the world. But it's the going into that makes the idea. You can't wait for a theory, but you have to have a theory.

LOUIS: As my grandma said, go know.

PRIOR: This angel. She's my favorite angel.

I like them best when they're statuary. They commemorate death but they suggest a world without dying. They are made of the heaviest things on earth, stone and iron, they weigh tons but they're winged, they are engines and instruments of flight.

This is the angel Bethesda. Louis will tell you her story.

LOUIS: Oh. Um, well, she was this angel, she landed in the Temple square in Jerusalem, in the days of the Second Temple, right in the middle of a working day she descended and just her foot touched earth. And where it did, a fountain shot up from the ground.

When the Romans destroyed the Temple, the fountain of Bethesda ran dry.

PRIOR: And Belize will tell you about the nature of the fountain, before its flowing stopped.

BELIZE: If anyone who was suffering, in the body or the spirit, walked through the waters of the fountain of Bethesda, they would be healed, washed clean of pain.

PRIOR: They know this because I've told them, many times. Hannah here told it to me. She also told me this:

HANNAH: When the Millennium comes . . .

PRIOR: Not the year two thousand, but the Capital M Millennium . . .

HANNAH: Right. The fountain of Bethesda will flow again. And I told him I would personally take him there to bathe. We will all bathe ourselves clean.

LOUIS: Not literally in Jerusalem, I mean we don't want this to have sort of Zionist implications.

BELIZE: Right on.

LOUIS: But on the other hand we *do* recognize the right of the state of Israel to exist.

BELIZE: But the West Bank should be a homeland for the Palestinians, and the Gaza Strip . . .

LOUIS: Well not *both* the Gaza Strip and the West Bank, I mean no one supports Palestinian rights more than I do but . . .

BELIZE : Oh yeah right, Louis, like not even the Palestinians are more devoted than . . .

PRIOR: I'm almost done.

The fountain's not flowing now, they turn it off in the winter, ice in the pipes. But in the summer it's a sight to see. I want to be around to see it. I plan to be. I hope to be.

This disease will be the end of many of us, but not nearly all, and the dead will be commemorated and will struggle on with the living, and we are not going away. We won't die secret deaths anymore. The world only spins forward. We will be citizens. The time has come.

Bye now.

You are fabulous creatures, each and every one.

And I bless you: *More Life.*

The Great Work Begins.

END OF PLAY

With a Little Help from My Friends

Angels in America, Parts One and Two, has taken five years to write, and as the work nears completion I find myself thinking a great deal about the people who have left their traces in these texts. The fiction that artistic labor happens in isolation, and that individual talents are the sole provenance of artistic accomplishment, is politically, ideologically charged and, in my case at least, repudiated by the facts.

While the primary labor on *Angels* has been mine (defensively, nervously, I hasten to shore up my claim to authorship), over two dozen people have contributed words, ideas, structures to these plays, including actors, directors, audiences, one-night stands, my former lover Mark Bronnenberg (to whom *Millennium Approaches* is dedicated) and many friends. Two people in particular—my closest friend, Kimberly T. Flynn (*Perestroika* is dedicated to her), and the man who commissioned *Angels* and helped shape it, Oskar Eustis—have had profound, decisive influences. Had I written these plays without the direct and indirect participation of my collaborators, the results would be entirely different and much the poorer for the deprivation—would, in fact, never have come to be.

We're in previews for *Perestroika*. It's roller-coaster time: nights when the audience loves it, nights when they love it too much, nights when they don't love it at all; nights when I'm exhilarated and nights when, during the intermissions, I crouch in outer stairwells and spin fantasies of vanishing from the face of the earth. There's no time more difficult for a playwright, at least not professionally, at least not for me. Narcissistic investment in every moment onstage occasions a crisis of overidentification. Each line that doesn't detonate with the force it possessed when I first heard it in the theatre-inside-my-head feels to me like a humiliation, a violation, a cause for wrath and despair. A life spent looking forward to repeated experiences of this undignified agony ceases, in previews, to have any appeal whatsoever.

We pay high prices for the maintenance of the myth of the Individual: we have no system of universal health care, we don't educate our children, we can't pass sane gun control laws, we elect presidents like Reagan, we hate and fear inevitable processes like aging and death, and on and on. Way down close to the bottom of the list of the evils Individualism visits on our culture are previewing playwrights suffering paroxysms of mortification and rage, caught up myopically, claustrophobically, sometimes catastrophically, in the dramas of their selves.

In the modern era it isn't enough to write; you must also be a Writer, and play your part as the agonist in a cautionary narrative in which you will fail or triumph, be in or out, hot or cold, ride the Wheel of Fortune (the medieval one, not the one with Vanna White). You become a character in a metadrama into which your own dramatizing has pitched you. The rewards can be fantastic, the punishment dismal; it's a zero-sum game, and its guarantor of value, its marker, is that you pretend you play it solo, preserving the myth that you alone are the wellspring of your creativity. It's a very popular myth. And through it your self attains the same status of rarity, of commodity (and it is a dubious distinction), as may be conferred upon the work that bears your name.

The success of *Millennium* made the rewrites of *Perestroika* excruciating. All summer I carried around Gore Vidal's wise words, written on the flyleaf of my journal: "What matters finally is not the world's judgment of oneself but one's own judgment of the world." This sentence had a talismanic power, though I knew that for me, finally, the world's judgment mattered mightily, and I shuddered to read Vidal's conclusion: "Any writer who lacks this final arrogance will not survive very long in America." There are many kinds of arrogance I don't lack, but that *final* one . . .

There's no point in pretending that *Angels in America* is the work of a self-effacing person. The grandiose side of my character is, I hope, reasonably balanced against an overly vigilant superego with a mean right hook. I decided when I started to write these plays five years ago to attempt something of ambition and size, even if that meant being vulnerable to accusations of having strayed too close to ambition's ugly twin, pretentiousness. Indeed pretentiousness and the willingness to risk being labeled pretentious are sins the commission of which most American writers I admire have been guilty, sometimes fleetingly, sometimes to a fault. Given the bloody opulence of this country's great and terrible history, given its newness and its grand improbability, its artists are bound to be tempted towards large gestures and big embraces—a proclivity de Tocqueville deplored as a national artistic trait nearly two hundred years ago. Melville, my favorite American writer, sounds inflated, even hysterical on occasion. It's the sound of the Individual ballooning, overreaching, a sound that attains its most glorious expression in Whitman. We are all children of "Song of Myself." And maybe in this spacious, under- and depopulated, as yet only lightly inscribed country, the Individual will finally expand to its unstable, insupportably swollen limits, and pop. (But here I risk pretentiousness, and an excess of optimism to boot—another American trait.)

Anyone interested in exploring alternatives to Individualism and the political economy it serves, capitalism, has to be willing to ask hard questions about the ego, both as abstraction and as exemplified in oneself. Bertolt Brecht, while he was still in Weimar-era Berlin, facing the possibility of participating in a socialist revolution, wrote a series of remarkable short plays, his Lehrstucke, or learning plays. The principle subject of these plays was the painful dismantling, as a revolutionary exigency, of the individual ego. Brecht's metaphor for this dismantling is death.

Brecht, who never tried to hide the dimensions of his own titanic personality, didn't sentimentalize the problems such personalities present, or the process of loss involved in letting go of the richness, and the riches, that accompany successful self-creation.

In his early days Brecht stole from other writers so brazenly that he could not possibly have intended to get away with it and must instead have been calling attention to an aspect of the act of writing: what the poststructuralists call "intertextuality," or what the courts sometimes call plagiarism. Brecht simultaneously claimed and mocked the identity he'd won for himself, "a great German writer," raising important questions about the means of literary production, challenging the sacrosanctity of the image of the solitary artist, and at the same time openly, ardently wanting to be recognized as a genius. That he was a genius is inarguably the case. For a man deeply committed to collectivity as an ideal and an achievable political goal, this blazing singularity was a mixed blessing at best and, at worst, an obstacle to praxis, to a blending of radical theory and practice.

In the lower right-hand corner of the title page of many of Brecht's plays you will find, in tiny print, a list of names under the heading "Collaborators." Sometimes these people contributed little, sometimes a great deal. One cannot help feeling that his collaborators, those tiny names, and the considerable labor the diminutive typography conceals, have gotten a bum deal. Many of these effaced collaborators—Ruth Berlau, Elisabeth Hauptmann, Margarete Steffin—were women. Gender is always an issue.

Playwrights who aspire to a theatre of political analysis and engagement must consider the life of Brecht and all its contradictory details. The contradictions do not point simply towards hypocrisy or bad faith, though they sometimes point to these. They also locate the most difficult and exciting complexities, pitfalls and radical potential the marriage of art and politics has to offer.

On the day last spring when the Tony nominations were being handed out, I left the glamorous room at Sardi's thinking gloomily that here was another source of anxiety, another obstacle to getting back to work rewriting *Perestroika*. In the lobby of the Sardi's building I was introduced to the producer Elizabeth McCann, who said to me: "I've been worried about how you were handling all this, till I read in that *New Yorker* piece you have an Irish woman in your life. Then I knew you were going to be fine." Ms. McCann was referring to Kimberly T. Flynn; an article in the *New Yorker* last year about *Angels in*

America described how certain features of our shared experience dealing with her prolonged health crisis, caused by a serious cab accident several years ago, had a major impact on the plays.

Kimberly and I met in 1978 when I was a student at Columbia and she was a student at Barnard; she worked on the crew of my first directorial effort, a production of Ben Jonson's *Bartholomew Fair*. We both participated in the antiapartheid movement at Columbia and joined a political theatre collective that struggled for a year before imploding. In the course of that year we became close friends.

Kimberly and I share Louisiana childhoods (she's from New Orleans, I grew up in Lake Charles); we share different but equally complicated, powerful religious traditions and a deep ambivalence towards those traditions; Left politics informed by liberation struggles (she as a feminist, I as a gay man) and by socialist and psychoanalytic theory; and a belief in the effectiveness of activism and the possibility of progress.

From the beginning Kimberly was my teacher. Though largely self-taught, she was more widely read than I was and she helped me make sense of both Freud and Marx far more thoroughly than I had previously been able to do. She introduced me, through her own explorations, to the writers of the Frankfurt School and their early attempts at synthesizing psychoanalysis and Marxism; and to Walter Benjamin, whom I first read at Kimberly's insistence, and whose importance for me rests primarily in his introduction into the "scientific" disciplines of Marx and Freud a Kabbalist-inflected mysticism and a dark, apocalyptic spirituality.

As both writer and talker Kimberly employs a rich variety of rhetorical strategies and effects, even while expressing deep emotion. She identifies this as an Irish trait; it's evident in O'Neill, Yeats, Beckett. This relationship to language, blended with Jewish and gay versions of the same strategies, is evident in my plays, in the ways my characters speak.

More pessimistic than I, Kimberly is much less afraid to look at the ugliness of the world. She tries to protect herself far less than I do, and consequently she sees more. She feels safest, she says, knowing the worst, while most people I know, myself included, would rather be spared and feel safer encircled protectively by a measure of obliviousness. She has both an analytic and an intuitive intelligence; she's capable of pulling things apart, teasing out fundamental concerns from their camouflage, and at the same time she is a talented synthesizer, able and willing to use her mind, her learning, her emotions, her lived experience, and finally to make imaginative leaps, to see the deeper connections between ideas and historical developments. Like all gifted teachers she approaches life as a student, endlessly eager to know. Through her example I learned to trust that such leaps can be made; I learned to admire them, in literature, in theory, in the utterances people make in newspapers. And certainly it was in part her example that made the labor of synthesizing disparate, seemingly unconnected things become, for me, the process of writing a play.

And for years now Kimberly has struggled with her health, which has been impaired because of injuries sustained in the accident; and I have struggled to help her, sometimes succeeding, sometimes failing; and it doesn't take much more than a passing familiarity with *Angels* to see how my life and my plays match up. It's always been easier talking about the way in which I used what we'd lived through to write *Angels* (even though I sometimes question the morality of the act, while at the same time considering it unavoidable if I was to write at all) than it has been to acknowledge the intellectual debt. People seem to be more interested in the story of the accident and its aftermath than in the intellectual genealogy of the work, the emotional life being privileged over the intellectual life in the business of making plays, and the two being regarded, incorrectly, as separable.

A great deal of what I understand about health issues comes from what Kimberly has endured and triumphed over, and the ways she has articulated those experiences. But *Angels* is more a result of our intellectual friendship than it is autobiography (which it really isn't at all). Over the years, and particularly in the last set of rewrites, Kimberly functioned as a dramaturg, and many of her suggestions for rewrites have been incorporated. Her contribution to *Angels* was as teacher, editor, adviser, not muse.

Perhaps other playwrights don't have similar relationships or similar debts; perhaps they have. In a wonderful, recently published collection of essays on creative partnerships, entitled *Significant Others* (Thames and Hudson), the contributors examine both healthy and deeply unhealthy versions of artistic interdependence in such couples as the Delaunays, Kahlo and Rivera, Hammett and Hellman, and Jasper Johns and Robert Rauschenberg—and in doing so strike forcefully at what the editors call "the myth of solitariness."

We have no words for the people to whom we are indebted. I call Oskar Eustis a dramaturg, sometimes a collaborator; but collaborator implies co-authorship and nobody knows what "dramaturg" implies. Oskar has an astonishing sensitivity to a writer's process, and an eye for thematic development born out of a profound acquaintance with literature and his great intelligence. Oskar and I share a romantic-ambivalent love for American history and a belief in what the character Louis Ironson calls "the prospect of some sort of radical democracy spreading outward and growing up." When I wrote in the acknowledgments for *Perestroika* that the plays began in conversation with Oskar, I meant both in actuality and in my mind. For a year before I started writing *Millennium*, and for every year during the process of writing *Angels*, I talked volumes with Oskar. Together, in dialogue, we created the optimistic heart of the plays. Every step of the play's development was passed by him, filtered through him. Oskar continues to be for me, intellectually and emotionally, what the developmental psychologists call "a secure base of attachment" (a phrase I learned from Kimberly).

George C. Wolfe became my dragon-slayer when I found the prospect of resuming work on *Perestroika* too daunting this spring. With his galvanic confidence, writer's insight and narrative clarity he swept the path clean for the play to find itself, its own identity distinct from Part One, as I believe it finally, finally has done. Many of the actors who have worked on the plays contributed ideas, lines, thoughts about cutting. Stephen Spinella, Ellen McLaughlin and Joe Mantello made wonderful suggestions during the period in which the script was being developed—a period that will end a week from now. Kathleen Chalfant rarely makes suggestions, but from the beginning the whole crowd of people she plays was written to the sounds of her voice and her majestic presence. Declan Donellan, who directed the play in London, has fed the process from his side of the Atlantic, phoning and faxing suggestions and ideas based on his inimitable sense of the theatrical event.

The play is indebted, too, to writers I've never met. It's ironic that Harold Bloom, in his introduction to Olivier Revault D'Allones' *Musical Variations on Jewish Thought*, provided me with a translation of the Hebrew word for "blessing"—"more life"—which subsequently became key to the heart of *Perestroika*. Harold Bloom is also the author of *The Anxiety of Influence*, his oedipalization of the history of Western Literature, which when I first encountered it years ago made me so anxious my analyst suggested I put it away. Recently I had the chance to meet Professor Bloom and, guilty over my appropriation, I fled from the encounter as one of Freud's *Totem and Taboo* tribesmen might flee from a meeting with that primal father, the one with the big knife. (I hope one day to meet Professor Bloom.)

The world howls without; it is at this moment a very terrible world—what the first character you meet in *Perestroika* calls an "inevident welter of fact, event, phenomenon, calamity." I have been blessed with remarkable friends, colleagues, comrades, collaborators: Together we organize the world for ourselves, or at least we organize our understanding of it; we reflect it, refract it, criticize it, grieve over its savagery; and we help each other to discern, amidst the gathering dark, paths of resistance, pockets of peace, and places from whence hope may be plausibly expected. Marx was right: The smallest divisible human unit is two people, not one; one is a fiction. From such nets of souls societies, the social world, human life springs. And also plays.

Tony Kushner
November 15, 1993

About the Author

Tony Kushner's plays include *A Bright Room Called Day* and his adaptation of Corneille's *The Illusion*. His work has been produced at the Mark Taper Forum, the New York Shakespeare Festival, New York Theatre Workshop, Hartford Stage Company, Berkeley Repertory Theatre and the Los Angeles Theatre Center, as well as other theatres around the country and abroad. He is the recipient of a 1990 Whiting Foundation Writers Award and playwriting and directing fellowships from the New York Foundation for the Arts, the New York State Council on the Arts and the National Endowment for the Arts. Mr. Kushner was born in Manhattan in 1956 and grew up in Lake Charles, Louisiana. He lives in New York City.

ABOUT THE PLAY

Angels in America, Parts One and Two, was commissioned by the Eureka Theatre Company through a special projects grant from the National Endowment for the Arts. The plays have been seen in San Francisco and at the Mark Taper Forum in Los Angeles. Part One: *Millennium Approaches* ran for a year in London at the Royal National Theatre. *Perestroika* opened there, in repertory with a revival of *Millennium*, on November 20, 1993. *Millennium* has been running at the Walter Kerr Theatre on Broadway since May 1993 and was joined by *Perestroika* on November 23, 1993.

Angels has received two Fund for New American Plays/American Express Awards, the Los Angeles Drama Critics' Circle Award for Best New Play of 1992 and the Outstanding Theatre Award from the Gay and Lesbian Alliance Against Defamation/Los Angeles. *Millennium* received the 1991 National Arts Club's Joseph Kesselring Award, the Bay Area Drama Critics Award for Best Play of 1991, the 1991 Will Glickman Award, the London *Evening Standard* Award for Best Play of 1992, the London Drama Critics' Circle Award for Best New Play, the 1993 Pulitzer Prize for Drama, the 1993 Tony Award for Best Play, and the New York Drama Critics' Circle and Drama Desk Awards for Best Play.